SLEEPY HOLLOW

SLEEPY HOLLOW

Children of the Revolution

KEITH R. A. DeCANDIDO

TITAN BOOKS

Sleepy Hollow: Children of the Revolution
Print edition ISBN: 9781783297740
E-book edition ISBN: 9781783297931

Published by Titan Books
A division of Titan Publishing Group Ltd.
144 Southwark Street, London SE1 0UP
www.titanbooks.com

First edition October 2014
10 9 8 7 6 5 4 3 2 1

A CIP catalogue record for this title is available from the British Library.

Printed and bound by CPI Group (UK) Ltd, Croydon, CR0 4YY

To Sterling, Jezebelle, and Louie, three noble cats.
While I was writing this book, the former two died and the latter
joined our home. All three enriched my life in so many ways, mostly
by lying around looking cute and demanding to be scritched.

SLEEPY HOLLOW

ONE

SLEEPY HOLLOW, NEW YORK

JANUARY 2014

THE GREAT CONTRADICTION of Ichabod Crane's life was that he was constantly surrounded by people, yet had never been more alone.

The number of things to which Crane had been forced to adjust since awakening in the early twenty-first century—subjectively mere moments after his death at the hands of an enemy soldier he'd beheaded in the late eighteenth century—were legion. At times, though, the adjustment that vexed him the most was the sheer number of *people* around him. In his previous life as a soldier, first for the British Regular Army and then for the Continental Army, he was an aristocrat. Rarely did he find himself surrounded by strangers, and such occasions were fleeting, and often on the battlefield.

Indeed, the number of people he *could* have been

surrounded by was negligible. The entirety of the colonies contained barely more than two thousand souls at the time of his alleged death. As the calendar changed from Anno Domini 2013 to 2014, Sleepy Hollow alone had an order of magnitude more people in it than the colonies had had in toto, and it was one of the smaller of what Lieutenant Mills had once called "bedroom communities" that dotted the Lower Hudson Valley, north of New York City.

Once he could go a full half year without encountering a single person with whom he was not at least acquainted enough to shake hands and exchange pleasantries. Now every day he was awash in strangers, wearing absurd clothing, occupied with pursuits Crane found impossible to fathom.

He took only small solace from the fact that those same folk would find his own pursuits even more baffling.

On this cold winter day he found himself drawn, as he often was, to Patriots Park, which lay on the border between Sleepy Hollow and the adjoining village to the south, Tarrytown. The park had been constructed around a monument to John Paulding, one of three Continental Army soldiers who captured a spy named John André. Crane recalled ＿＿＿ ＿nt, though he'd been elsewhere at the ＿＿＿ was fairly certain that the actual capture ＿＿＿, a confederate of Benedict Arnold, was in ＿＿＿ uarter of a mile from this spot. His months in the twenty-first century, however, had taught him that history only remembered his time dimly when anyone bothered to remember it at all.

The park was quiet on this winter afternoon, for which Crane was grateful. Snow covered much of the grass, though the smoothly paved oval-shaped passageways were cleared. He heard the sound of children across the thoroughfare known as the Broad Way (an odd appellation, as it was not significantly wider than any of the other nearby boulevards). The Paulding School was just letting out, having apparently concluded the day's lessons.

Crane strode, lost in thought, past the monument and wandered around the pathway that took him onto one of the two stone bridges that overlooked the brook.

One of the few people in the park was a woman of Oriental descent, who was strolling with a very small dog of indeterminate breed. The woman wore plastic spectacles of the type that were fashionable in this era, and wore an animal-hide jacket that seemed insufficient protection against the cold, particularly given the number of frays and holes that dotted her dungarees.

Having learned the hard way that the people of this century did not always appreciate a simple greeting, Crane said nothing to the woman.

She was less restrained, to his surprise and delight. "I *love* that coat. Where did you *find* such a hot vintage piece?"

"This topcoat was a gift." It was, Crane had found, the easiest method of explaining his clothing.

"Ooh, *love* the accent. And I bet it keeps you warm—the coat, not the accent, I mean. This winter has been just *awful*." The dog chose this moment to make a detailed olfactory survey of the bridge.

"Has it?" Crane smiled. "I've endured far worse winters in this very region. Indeed, I find this particular season to be quite bracing by comparison."

"If you say so, but I just wanna go back home to Cali."

"Who is this Cally you speak of?"

"Not who, hot stuff, *where*. California? That's where I'm from?"

"I'm afraid I haven't had the privilege of visiting."

The woman glanced at her dog, who was still attempting to sniff the entire bridge, then smiled back at Crane. "I *adore* the way you talk. Anyhow, I'm from L.A., and it's *always* summer there. Much better than this. I've been freezing my *ass* off."

Crane resisted the urge to glance at the woman's posterior to see if it was still attached, as the last time he heard that particular phrase his doing so had resulted in an open-handed blow to his cheek. Instead, he simply said, "It amazes me that the people of this time, with such wondrousness as central heating and insulation, still wax rhapsodic on the subject of how awful the cold is. But then it seems the denizens of this century are never happier than when they're complaining."

"This century? Dude, you can't be *that* much older than me."

Crane's smile widened. "You have no idea, miss."

The dog chose that moment to continue its examination on Crane's boots.

Chuckling, the woman said, "Guess Puddles likes your boots as much as I do. Were they a gift, too?"

"Indeed." Crane stared down at Puddles. "I hope your pet's name isn't indicative of how he intends to express his affection for my footwear."

"Nah, he only pees on trees. Only dog in the world that avoids fire hydrants. That's why I like to bring him here. Well, that, and it's a nice park. I love the history, y'know? The monuments to the people who died in the wars."

Crane nodded. Near another entrance to the park sat three monuments, one each for those local residents who died in the three of the wars that plagued the world in the previous century.

"Although I don't think it's entirely fair," the woman added.

The list of things that Crane considered unfair was considerable, but in the interests of politeness, rather than volunteer suggestions for what she meant, he instead asked, "What isn't?"

"Well, the brook—it's named André Brook. Why name it after the bad guy?"

"One wonders why it is named at all. The obsession with nomenclature is mind-boggling. I recall—" Crane stopped, reminding himself that actually stating he was from another time tended to send conversations in a direction that ended poorly for him. "There was a time when this brook had no name, nor had it need for one."

"Well, I'd rather it had no name. I mean, c'mon, André was the one who was the friggin' *spy*. Paulding gets the statue *and* the school named after him, and André gets the brook. What about Williams and van Wart?"

"I believe Militiaman Paulding receives the lion's share of the accolades because he was the only one of the three who captured Major André who was literate. It was he who read the papers André carried, and therefore found him out as a traitor."

"Huh." The woman considered Crane's words. "I didn't know that. Go fig'."

Puddles then decided to start running toward the other end of the bridge, eliminating the entirety of the slack on the lead the woman used to guide him. As she allowed herself to be pulled along, the woman waved with her free hand. "Well, it was nice meeting you! Happy new year!"

"To you as well, madam!" Crane even waved back to her, finding her conversation to be oddly stimulating, despite her unnecessary complaints about the cold.

Crane leaned on the side of the bridge, listening to the hypnotic rustle of the brook as it flowed across the channel that served as the border between the two townships.

For a moment, he closed his eyes, enjoying the noise of the water. With his eyes shut, he imagined the sound of meat as it cooked on a pan over a fire.

That, in turn, made him realize that he had not yet had his afternoon repast. His stomach made odd noises as a further reminder. With a sigh, he opened his eyes—

—only to find himself no longer in Patriots Park.

He had not moved, yet he stood in an expansive forest. It was darkest night. No sign of the sun peeked through the gnarled, wizened trees that choked the landscape for as far as Crane's eyes could see. The air had transformed from the crisp cool of a Sleepy Hollow afternoon to heavy and thick. Taking a breath had gone from bracing to laboring, and he found it difficult to stand upright.

No stars dotted the sky, yet Crane could spy a full moon through one of the few gaps amid the branches. Not that Crane needed further proof, but it was early January and the next full moon wasn't until mid-month. This meant either he'd traveled forward in time—again—or this was a magical realm.

All things considered, the latter seemed the most likely. He'd received visions in dreams from Katrina, and both he and Lieutenant Mills had received waking visions from various sources, from Katrina to the evil Moloch to his friend the Sin-Eater, Henry Parrish. This was very much like those, and Crane was getting rather impatient with them.

"Whoever is responsible, show yourself!"

Crane considered exploring the region. But no, he'd been taken to this place for a reason. If this was the spot he was brought to, he was supposed to be here. If not, he was hardly about to oblige his host by stumbling about in the dark.

Again, he cried out, "Show yourself!"

Suddenly, he was no longer in the forest, but in the van Brunt mansion, sharing a drink with Abraham van Brunt. They were awaiting the arrival of a messenger who would provide them with their next task to perform on behalf of the Continental Congress.

"I have to say, Ichabod, this brandy is simply awful. Where did you find it?"

Without thinking, Crane responded now as he had then: "Your liquor cabinet, Abraham."

"What a pity, I was hoping I had better taste than this."

Crane shook his head, trying to force himself to speak to his best friend once again. They had shared this drink several nights prior to when Katrina van Tassel broke off her engagement with van Brunt and declared her love for Crane. That action sundered their friendship, and led to van Brunt selling his very soul, allying himself with evil to enact revenge on Crane and Katrina both.

But van Brunt and his sitting room disappeared then, replaced by General Washington and an outdoor location. Crane stood now with the general and several of his aides at the site of a massacre near Albany, New York, surrounded by torn tents, ruined fires, rotting food, broken weaponry, and corpses that had been burned in a manner not possible by any weapon Crane was familiar with.

"I have been expecting something like this since Trenton," Washington said. "We both won and lost that day."

Before Crane could even respond, the vista altered yet again. This time it was the Masonic cell where he, Lieutenant Mills, and Captain Irving had trapped Death, the Horseman of the Apocalypse, who was embodied by van Brunt after he felt himself betrayed. Mills's deceased comrade, Lieutenant Brooks, was speaking for the Horseman, taunting him.

"I took *you*! I took you on the battlefield! I slayed your Mason brethren, I hung their heads like lanterns! I killed her partner, and I *will* kill *you*."

Another change in scene, this time standing over the golem that Katrina had given to Jeremy. The doll had been imbued with tremendous destructive power in order to fulfill its mission to protect their son. Crane had been forced to kill the creature with a blade stained with his own blood.

Again Crane spoke the words he spoke to the golem as it died on the sands of the strange carnival, while holding its misshapen hand: "You have endured enough pain. Bear it no more."

Then another change, to a bitter cold winter day

at Fort Carillon, which had just been taken by the Continental Army. Crane stood with Caleb Whitcombe and Henry Knox, tasked with moving several of the fort's cannons to Boston.

Whitcombe was saying, "Are you sure this is wise, Knox? This place was hardly a model of efficiency before old Captain Delaplace surrendered. Shall we make it less fortified by taking their cannon?"

"We've been over this," Knox replied now as he had in 1775. "Boston is of far more import than Two Lakes."

Crane smiled at the use of the English translation of the region, which the Iroquois called Ticonderoga—and then the scene changed yet again, to a meeting of the Sons of Liberty in New York, led by Marinus Willett. Crane sat in the gallery, surrounded both by members of the Sons and those like himself who were sympathetic. Next to him sat van Brunt.

Willett was speaking: "The regulars are tearing down the liberty poles almost as fast as we may put them up. Perhaps it is time to attempt a different tactic."

Another man, whose name Crane never did learn, said, "No! Our poles of liberty will be like the heads of the hydra! If they tear down one, we put up two to take its place!"

Willett smiled. "Very well."

Then he was back in the forest, alone. A half-moon now illuminated the night sky through the gnarled trees.

Crane's pulse raced when he saw that Katrina now stood before him. The red hair and magnificently steely features of his wife was the most glorious sight he could imagine. For months, he had suffered through life in a bizarre new century, conscripted to fight a war he barely even understood, while the one thing that grounded him, that kept him from completely succumbing to utter madness, was the knowledge that Katrina was trapped in purgatory and there was a possibility that she might be freed and they would, at last, be reunited.

He'd seen visions of her before, caught glimpses, been given messages, and every time it happened, his heart broke a little bit more.

Like so much of what he'd seen since coming to this place, Katrina was ever-changing. At first she was dressed in the elegant gown she wore the night she ended her engagement to van Brunt, but then that changed to the simple Mennonite dress and bonnet she wore when first they met, and then the nurse's raiment she was clothed in on the battlefield, including the day of his fateful encounter with the Horseman.

She stood a yard away from him.

"Katrina!" He moved toward her, but always she remained a yard away.

Urgently, she cried out, "You must retrieve the medal you were awarded!"

And then she once again disappeared, leaving Crane alone in the forest, forcing him to lose her all over again.

"Katrina!" he cried more loudly this time.

He started running toward where she had been, but suddenly he found himself surrounded by more trees that cut off every avenue of escape.

No longer did he see an image of a person from his past, nor could he even see the trees, though the half-moon still illuminated the sky. Then, suddenly, there were eight half-moons.

"Katrina!"

"Dude, who the hell's Katrina?"

Whirling around, Crane found himself blinded by the sunlight. Shading his eyes with his hands, he blinked the odd-colored shapes out of his eyes and eventually focused on the woman with the dog from earlier, who was gazing upon him with obvious concern. She was still walking Puddles, who was now making high-pitched barking noises at Crane's feet.

Crane shook his head. "My apologies, miss, I did not mean to—" He took a breath.

The look of concern modulated into a smile. "It's okay. I've been there, too. You stand here, sun shining on your face, the sound of the brook flowing, and you just go all daydreamy, am I right?"

"So it would seem," Crane said lamely. While he was sure this young woman had ample charms in her own right, he needed to speak to Lieutenant Mills immediately.

She put a hand out. "Well, my name isn't Katrina, it's Lianne, and I came back here because I realized I didn't introduce myself. My mom taught me better than that, especially when the other person in the conversation is as polite as you are. Seriously, you're the nicest guy I've met since I moved here for college."

Crane immediately took Lianne's hand and bent forward in a proper bow. "The pleasure has been entirely mine, Miss Lianne. My name is Ichabod Crane, and I remain at your service." He returned her hand to her and stood upright. "I'm afraid, however, that my—my daydream has reminded me of a pressing matter to which I must immediately attend. If you will excuse me."

Lianne was just holding the hand he'd kissed, in a state of befuddlement that Crane might have found amusing under different circumstances.

Giving her another bow and taking her stunned silence for assent to his request to be excused, Crane turned and headed off the bridge down the stone path that would take him to the Broad Way. Reaching into the pocket of the coat that Lianne had so admired, he pulled out the device that was referred to as a "cell phone." He assumed the modifier "cell" was a joke referring to how much modern humanity was imprisoned by such devices, as it seemed that the citizens of the twenty-first century relied on them to an appalling degree.

Still, Crane could not help but be impressed by

the accomplishment. By simply entering a prear-
ranged code into this object that appeared to be a
simple block of refined metal, Crane could, theo-
retically, communicate with anyone in the world.
It was a capacity that Crane found unimaginable,
and he often mused on what the Continental Army
could have done with such communicative powers.

Then again, the Regular Army would have had
access to same. If nothing else, they might have
communicated to Lord George Germain that Jonas
Bronck's River could not accommodate a vessel any
larger than a rowboat, which would have saved his
lordship a certain amount of embarrassment when
he ordered gunboats to sail up that river passage.

Crane managed to navigate the phone's code system to connect himself to the lieutenant.

Abigail Mills answered after only one sounding
off of the phone's bell. "Talk fast, Crane, I'm in the
middle of a call with the ADA about the Ippolito
case."

"Who is this Ippolito gentleman?"

"Before your time—Ippolito's a guy Corbin and
I busted for B-and-E. The case is finally going to
trial after a ton of delays, so I'm going over my testimony with Czierniewski."

Crane only followed about half of what Mills
said, but he didn't bother to inquire further, as he
had more pressing matters to discuss. "I need to
see you immediately, Lieutenant. There is another
crisis brewing, though I'm afraid the nature of said

crisis remains a mystery that you and I must unravel."

"Which means it's another day ending in Y for us Witnesses," Mills said dryly.

Crane frowned. "Every day ends in—" He sighed. "Ah, yes, I see. Very droll."

"Look, I've got at least another ten minutes with Czierniewski. Why don't I meet you across the street in fifteen?"

"Very well."

By this time, Crane was walking down the Broad Way and headed for the armory that the local constabulary had converted to an archive. After the previous sheriff, August Corbin, was murdered, his personal files were sent there. Corbin had collected a great deal of information about the supernatural happenings in and around Sleepy Hollow, so Crane and Mills had, with the blessing of Corbin's replacement, Captain Frank Irving, taken over the armory as their de facto headquarters in the ongoing battle against the mystical forces that were arrayed against them.

Irving had proven a valuable ally, as had Jenny Mills, the lieutenant's sister, who had aided Corbin in his quest to learn all he could about the battle they were all enmeshed in. Miss Jenny had taken to referring to the armory as "the Batcave," a reference that Crane had found impenetrable.

The armory itself was one of the few structures that remained from Crane's time. According to the histories he'd read over the past few months, the village received an influx of new residents both rich and poor after the invention of the railroad, and another after the invention of the automobile. Both waves of population expansion were accompanied by new construction, much of which replaced the existing farmhouses. By the turn of the twentieth century, the agrarian village that Crane knew was all but gone.

A few exceptions remained, such as the Old Dutch Church, which had already been standing for a century when Crane first visited it, and this very armory, in which several of the strategies enacted in the Battle of Lexington and Concord had been plotted.

It was a short, brisk walk up the Broad Way to Beekman Avenue, the thoroughfare on which both police headquarters and the armory lay.

He entered the latter, nodding to the uniformed officer who sat behind a metal desk reading a copy of the *Journal News,* the newspaper that serviced this vicinity.

"Afternoon, Mr. Crane."

Crane blinked, not recalling having been introduced to this particular constable. "Good afternoon. I'm afraid you have the advantage of me—" He glanced at the nameplate on the woman's chest. "—Officer Marble. Have we met?"

She folded the newspaper and put it down on the

desk. "No, but trust me, everyone knows who you are."

"Do they?" Crane was a bit nonplussed by that.

Marble snorted. "C'mon, Corbin gets killed, Abbie decides *not* to go to D.C., and you and her spend all your time holed up in here. Plus, she ain't been in the rotation, and Irving's covering both your asses." She grinned. "It's a small town, and we don't have that much to talk about, least till baseball season starts."

"Ah, you are a fan of baseball, then? I'm afraid I did not acquire a taste for the sport until Lieutenant Mills took me to a game."

"Yeah, well, don't let her fool you into thinking the Mets are a *good* team. You wanna see *real* baseball, go to Yankee Stadium."

"I will bear that in mind," Crane said diplomatically, though he followed only part of what Marble said. "If you'll excuse me."

"You bet." She picked the paper back up. "Good luck with whatever you guys are doing back there."

Crane reached into his coat pocket to retrieve the metal band that contained the ever-growing collection of keys he'd accumulated. It took him a moment to find the configuration that matched that of this particular door, and then he allowed himself ingress.

A few minutes after he settled into one of the chairs of dubious comfort that had been placed in the room, he heard Mills conversing with Officer Marble. They seemed to be discoursing on the subject of gentlemen by the names of Harvey, Tanaka, Sabathia, and Wright, as well as someone with the appellation "Ayrod."

Finally, Mills joined him, shaking her head. "I don't know who's crazier, Liz Marble for thinkin' the Yanks aren't gonna suck again this year or Johnny Ippolito for not pleading out. If he'd just taken the plea that Czierniewski offered him when Corbin and I busted him a year and a half ago, he'd already be back on the streets." She blew out a breath. "So what's our latest mystery?"

After providing Mills with a précis of his vision, Crane concluded with "I can only surmise that Katrina was forced to keep our contact brief as a consequence of my sojourn to visit her in purgatory."

Mills nodded. "Yeah, Moloch's probably keeping the bonds pretty tight on her after that. So what medal do you need to retrieve?"

"I've no idea." Crane shook his head and rose to his feet. He told Mills the story while seated, but now he felt restless. "I received no medal from either the Crown or the colonies."

"Did she give you any kind of hint?"

Testily, Crane said, "The sum total of her words to me were what I quoted to you: 'You must retrieve the medal you were awarded.'"

"Maybe it wasn't just words. What else did you see?"

"I saw flashes of people who are in some way involved in our conflict, either present-day or during the war: General Washington, van Brunt, you, Moloch, and—" Crane blinked. "Wait—of course! I also saw Willett!"

"Who's that?"

Crane shook his head. "Marinus Willett, the leader of the Sons of Liberty. The Continental Congress awarded ten of us with the Congressional Cross. It was a citation for bravery in the struggle against the Crown. It was one of several decorations that were distributed—they also issued elegant swords to some soldiers, as well as the Fidelity Medallion, which John Paulding and his compatriots received after capturing Major André."

Mills smiled. "Kinda surprised Mr. Photographic Memory forgot that. What happened to the cross after you died?"

Tartly, Crane said, "Mr. Photographic Memory did not forget it, because he was never issued the cross. While the Congress did declare that ten of us were to receive the honor, the actual crosses were commissioned to be created by a French silversmith. But they had not been completed by the time of my semi-fatal encounter with the Horseman."

"I like 'semi-fatal.' Okay, so usually when someone's awarded a medal posthumously, it goes to a family member."

Crane shook his head. "Hardly an option. Katrina was on the run after she cast her spell upon my corpse, and our son was not publicly known to be my heir." Crane shuddered involuntarily. The recent revelation that Katrina had birthed a son by him had shaken him to his very core. She herself had been unaware of the pregnancy until after Crane's battle with the Horseman. Katrina had left young Jeremy in the care of trusted comrades, but after they were killed, he was raised in an orphanage. "I'm afraid the only other family I had was my father. I doubt the nascent United States government would have issued such a citation to a member of the British aristocracy who disowned the recipient of that citation when he switched sides."

"'Here's a medal your dead son got for rebelling.' Yeah, probably not, no." Mills sighed. "All right, I think the first thing we need to do is find out everything we can about the Congressional Cross. Who else got them?"

"I'm afraid I couldn't say. Marinus Willett, van Brunt, and I were informed of our honors together after the fact. I was never informed of the full roster of ten."

"Too bad." She went over to the laptop computer in order to utilize the invisible library that was the Internet.

After several manipulations of the keyboard, Mills found herself on a page that provided some information. "Looks like that silversmith you mentioned was named Gaston Mercier, and he finished the crosses in 1785. They were shipped to the

United States. George Washington awarded them to the surviving recipients or to their families."

Crane shook his head. "As we've established, that is not applicable to all who received it. Does this webbed page provide a list?"

"*Web* page, and there's only one other name besides Willett and van Brunt: Tench Tilghman." She looked up. "What kind of parent names their kid 'Tench'?" Then she shook her head. "And why am I asking the person whose parents named him 'Ichabod'?"

Crane raised an eyebrow. "In fact, Lieutenant, my given name derives from the Book of Samuel. As for Mr. Tilghman, I'm afraid I never met him, though I do know that he was one of Washington's most trusted lieutenants."

She leaned back in her chair. "Well, there isn't much online about these crosses. I'll keep digging, but if that's all Katrina gave us, I'm not sure what else we can do."

"Indeed. I love Katrina more than life itself, Lieutenant, but with each passing day I realize that I knew her far less than I should have. We can only hope that my ignorance does not prove fatal for us all."

TWO

New York, New York

JANUARY 2014

BEFORE THE ACCIDENT, Frank Irving had paid very little attention to the Americans with Disabilities Act of 1990.

He was aware of it, certainly. If nothing else, when he was a uniformed rookie in the New York Police Department, his sergeant would sometimes task him with ticketing duty, telling him to paper cars that violated parking ordinances. He often wrote citations for vehicles parked in handicapped spots without proper tags or ones that blocked the lips in sidewalks to accommodate wheelchairs and strollers. And he was occasionally guilty of using the elevators in the subways when he just didn't feel like climbing the stairs.

But it wasn't until after the accident, after Macey was released from the hospital, after the doctors made it clear that she would never walk again, that Irving was able to truly appreciate the kindness that Congress had done his family with that law.

Macey herself took it for granted, which was easy for her, not having been born yet when the law passed. If Irving had been confined to a wheelchair when he was Macey's age back in the 1980s, he'd have had a much harder time of it: fewer elevators and ramps, fewer lips in the sidewalks, fewer parking spots set aside, and so on.

Then again, he'd been thinking a lot lately about how things had changed over the years. Having a displaced Revolutionary War soldier in his life had that effect. . . .

He and his teenage daughter were working their way up Fifth Avenue toward the ground-floor entrance to the Metropolitan Museum of Art that sat opposite East Eighty-First Street, passing the street artists and food and drink vendors that dotted the crowded sidewalk.

"Here we go, Little Bean," he said with a smile as he held the large metal door open for her. "I ever tell you that my earliest memories are of coming here?"

"Only a thousand times, Dad." Macey grinned indulgently. They went through this routine every time he brought her to the Met.

"You sure?" Irving asked with mock confusion. "I really told you about the time I was four years old?"

"*Yes*, Dad. You don't remember the whole trip,

just quick images like pictures. Standing in the main entrance, looking at a Rembrandt, staring down at all the pennies in the wishing well at the Temple of Dendur . . ."

"And the pigeons, don't forget the pigeons." Irving shrugged out of his coat, then helped Macey slide out of hers as they got in the coat-check line. "Dive-bombing me on the steps. It was like being in an Alfred Hitchcock movie. But even after that, I've been coming back here my whole life."

Macey smiled. "Didn't you tell me that you were the only cop in your precinct who had a membership to the museum?"

"Yeah, I was. Least I only made the mistake of asking the guys to come with me once." Cops and art generally didn't mix, and Irving took some serious ribbing after making that request. "Took me ten years to get them to stop calling me Picasso."

Once they checked their coats, they went to the membership desk and got the stickers with the Met's logo and the date. Wearing those on their shirts would permit them access to the museum for the rest of the day. While waiting for the elevator, Irving asked his daughter, "Where you wanna visit first?"

"Can we go to the Astor Court? One of the kids in the anime club went there, and I'm dying to see it!"

Irving frowned. "When did you join the anime club?"

"Like, forever ago, Dad. Remember, I went to that Miyazaki marathon?"

"Sure, right," Irving said quickly, though he recalled no such thing. He silently admonished himself for not paying near enough attention to his daughter's life and made a mental note to look up the name Miyazaki later to make sure his oeuvre was suitable for a teenager.

Murphy's Law being what it was, the Astor Court was all the way on the other end of the museum, an edifice that took up four city blocks. They took the elevator to the first floor, then moved slowly through the Greek sculpture, the main lobby with its high ceilings, wooden benches, and large crowds, then through the Egyptian wing before reaching another elevator.

When they went through the lobby, Macey noticed the much longer line for the coat check up here, and grinned. "See? There *are* benefits to being crippled."

Irving winced. He and his ex-wife, Cynthia, had gone to great lengths to never use the word *crippled* in Macey's presence, so naturally their daughter had decided one day to embrace the term. Part of it was an attempt at empowerment, something Irving could get behind. Certainly lots of the people he came up with in the neighborhood would embrace racial slurs for their own use, not to mention gay people similarly embracing *queer*. But Irving also had a sneaking suspicion that Macey used the word precisely because it made her parents uncomfortable. Just a little something to remind him that, whatever else she'd been through, Macey was still a teenager.

The elevator deposited them on the second floor right opposite the moon gate, the circular entryway to the Astor Court. First opened in 1981, the space was a re-creation of a Chinese garden, with a small body of water with koi swimming about, several plants, a small gazebo, several rock sculptures, and a skylight. Irving's first visit had been the year it opened, when he was thirteen.

Even at its most crowded, the place exuded calm.

Since the accident, Irving had gotten in the habit of walking behind Macey. At first, it was to push her wheelchair, but even after she started manipulating the chair herself, he remained behind her in order to keep an eye on her.

But halfway through the moon gate, he stopped, unable to continue forward.

It took Macey a moment to notice, and then she glanced back over her shoulder. "Dad?"

"Sorry, Little Bean, I just—" He shook his head and then finally went the rest of the way in, staring at the rock gardens and plants and simple-yet-ornate window designs and floor patterns.

Macey wheeled herself down the ramp onto the main part of the floor. "You okay, Dad?" she asked as he followed her.

"I just realized that I haven't been here since—since the accident."

"Why not?"

"I don't know, I—" He smiled ruefully. "This used to be my refuge. Back when I was a kid, I used to come up here to get away from it all. Whenever I was having problems in school or with my family or with the kids in the neighborhood, I'd come here. It was always quiet and peaceful, and it helped me make sense of things. After I joined the force, I came here a lot, too."

"By yourself, I take it?" Macey grinned when she asked the question.

Irving chuckled, grateful for the tension release of his daughter's teasing. "Yeah, by myself. Helped me deal with some stuff. And every time I came here, I felt better. Until the accident."

Macey wheeled the chair around so that she could put her hand on his. "Dad, I'm fine. I mean, I'm not *fine*, but I'm okay."

"I know that, Little Bean, but I didn't know that when I came here. You were still in the hospital, the doctors didn't know if you'd ever walk again—they weren't even sure how far up your body you'd be paralyzed."

Now Macey's face fell. "I didn't know that."

This time Irving broke the tension for his daughter. "Yeah, well, you were on the really high-quality painkillers at that point. You were having trouble remembering your own name."

She grinned. "So what happened when you came here?"

"It still didn't make sense. This place always made me feel better before, helped me get my thoughts in order, but when you were hurt—" He shook his head again. "Then I stopped coming. Didn't even realize it until now."

Irving went over to one of the places where you could sit, and just took in the peace. Anxiety over the accident, over what might happen to his little girl, overwhelmed that peace last time.

Today, the peace was swimming upstream against a headless soldier who'd murdered a colleague before Irving had helped capture him. The peace fought against witches and ghosts and time-displaced revolutionaries. The peace struggled to excise the threat to life, limb, and sanity that he had been facing from the second he transferred to Sleepy Hollow to replace a man who'd been beheaded.

He'd been a police officer his entire adult life, an NYPD cop for most of that. Yet he had never encountered a headless corpse until he took what was supposed to be a cushy position in the suburbs. Sleepy Hollow had had more murders in the past four months than in the previous twenty years.

And so for the second time in a row, and the second time ever, the Astor Court failed to provide the solace that Frank Irving had sought every time he'd come here since he was a teenager.

With a sigh, he rose to his feet.

Macey was still enjoying the quietude, and so he let her have it, standing off to the side until she was ready to go.

"Okay," she finally said after she had spent several seconds staring down at the fish in the pond, "where next?"

"How 'bout the American Wing?"

Shrugging, Macey said, "Sure."

Once, the American Wing had been a separate building just to the north of the museum. A courtyard separated them, but it wasn't long before that courtyard was enclosed. That was all before Irving's time, but he imagined that going outside to check out the American Wing probably wasn't any fun in winter.

Irving hadn't been over to that part of the museum in some time, not since they'd remodeled. The courtyard had been completely redone so that it was one big flat marble surface instead of a multilayered garden. Aesthetically, he didn't like it; as the parent of a teenager in a wheelchair, he loved it.

"Oooooh!" Macey said as she wheeled past the large glass door that led to Arms & Armor. "Can we go there?"

Shuddering, Irving said, "Maybe later." Swords and armor were the stuff of nightmares for him of late.

Of course, it was those same nightmares that drew him to the American Wing. They went through the façade of the former stand-alone building and found a computer terminal that provided an interactive map of the section. Irving was particularly interested in what they had from the time of the American Revolution.

"Why do you care about *that*, Dad?" Macey sounded understandably confused.

"Just curious," he said lamely, finding that most of the art from 1770 to 1800—what he'd started thinking of as "the Crane period"—was in one room, plus some other items in the huge vault of decorative arts that they'd collected at the museum.

The gallery in question was on the second floor. They went up in a glass-enclosed elevator that Macey decided was the coolest thing ever.

En route to that room, they came through the gallery that included Emanuel Leutze's famous portrait of George Washington crossing the Delaware River. A tour was in that room at the time, and Macey slowly wheeled her way through the crowd, all of whom quickly cleared a path for her to get through.

The tour guide was saying, "While Washington did indeed cross the Delaware on Christmas night in 1776, it's pretty much impossible for it to have looked anything like this. For starters, while it was a full moon that night, it wasn't *that* bright. By the time dawn rose, they were already en route to Trenton, not still crossing. They went across at about three in the morning. It was raining that night; the horses and field guns came across by ferry. The stars-and-stripes flag Washington's men are carrying wasn't in use yet. He would've had the Grand Union Flag, which had stripes, but no stars. And, the real biggie, there's just no way Washington could've stood like that in the boat without falling into the river."

The crowd laughed at that. So did Macey as they went into the next gallery over, which had paintings by Ralph Earl, Charles Willson Peale, John Trumbull, Gilbert Stuart, and others, many of whom had studied abroad and then returned to the newly formed United States to provide portraits of the heroes of the revolution.

A part of Irving half expected to see a portrait of Crane present, but he was spared that.

"Okay, that's just *weird*." Macey was staring at another portrait of George Washington, this one just of the first president standing near a tree.

"What is it?"

"He's pointing at the door."

Irving laughed. Washington was, indeed, pointing across his body with his right arm toward the entrance to the gallery. Perpendicular to that portrait was one of someone named Marinus Willett. Irving had never heard of the man who, according to the placard that he bent over to read, was a leader of the Sons of Liberty, negotiated treaties with the Muscogee tribe, and was appointed mayor of New York in 1807.

Macey followed Irving's gaze to the placard. "They appointed mayors? That isn't right."

"Aren't they teaching you stuff at school?" Irving asked with a chuckle. "New York mayors were appointed until 1834."

"That sucks."

"That's the great thing about this country, Little Bean—we adjust. Remember, you and I wouldn't have been considered people when the Constitution was signed."

"Yeah, I *know*, Dad," Macey said in her best *duh* voice. "They do teach us *some* stuff."

Irving smiled at his daughter, then read the rest of the placard. "Looks like Willett got two awards from the Continental Congress before they made him mayor. That sword he's holding in the painting is one."

Pointing at the display case to the left of the portrait, Macey said, "Not *just* in the painting."

"Yeah, that's the same sword." Irving was impressed with the level of detail that Earl, the artist, had put into the painting, as the sword Willett held on the canvas was a perfect match for the short sword in the case Macey was pointing at.

Now Macey peered at the placard. "What's the other one he won?"

"Something called the Congressional Cross." He straightened. "Says they've got that one, too, but it's on the mezzanine with the other decorative arts stuff. Wanna check it out?"

"Sure!"

Irving hadn't expected the enthusiasm, but then

he realized that it required a trip to the mezzanine, which meant another ride in the "totally awesome" glass elevator.

Unfortunately, the Luce Center, which housed Willett's Congressional Cross, was made up of forty-five floor-to-ceiling glass cases crammed fairly close together. It was hard for Macey to navigate through them. They also got sidetracked by the many different objects on display, including some very interesting everyday items. Macey in particular found it fascinating. "This is really cool. You don't think of historical people as having *stuff*, y'know?"

Thinking about Crane and his aversion to ever changing his clothes, Irving decided not to comment.

Eventually, they found where the Congressional Crosses were supposed to be. The case itself was empty, though the placard said that there were supposed to be two such, which were awarded to ten heroes of the American Revolution who'd displayed conspicuous bravery. A second placard in a different typeface claimed that the two crosses were being cleaned.

A fist of ice clenched Irving's heart when he read the name of the other person besides Willett whose medal was supposed to be on display: Abraham van Brunt.

Once, Irving knew, van Brunt had been Crane's closest friend. Both were aristocrats who sided with the colonies over the crown. Both also loved the same woman. Katrina van Tassel was engaged to van Brunt, but she loved Crane. When van Brunt found out, he went a little crazy, and Moloch took advantage of that craziness to make van Brunt into one of the Horsemen of the Apocalypse.

At times, he was seriously tempted to tell that story to Reverend Boland so he could use it to illustrate the value of following the Tenth Commandment. Covet your neighbor's wife, have your best friend turned into one of the harbingers of the apocalypse . . .

"You okay, Dad?"

Irving looked down at his daughter. "I'm fine, Little Bean, just got reminded of some stuff from work."

"Well, stop it. You're out with me," Macey said primly. "You shouldn't be thinking about work, just about making your daughter happy. Like letting her ride that awesome elevator again."

Irving grinned. "Sounds like a plan."

THREE

TRENTON, NEW JERSEY

DECEMBER 1776

LIEUTENANT COLONEL JOHANN Rall, the commandant of the Hessian regiment that occupied Trenton on behalf of the British Crown, had received two communiqués, both of which filled him with a sense of dread.

The first had been brought to him by one of his regiment commanders, Lieutenant Colonel Balthasar Brethauer. Rall broke the seal and read over the missive, sighing the entire time.

"I take it that the news is not good?" Brethauer asked dryly.

"You surmise correctly, Colonel. Major General von Donop sends his deepest regrets, but General Grant has denied my request for some British troops to supplement our own."

Brethauer made a *tch* noise and tugged on his waistcoat. "The Geordies hired us to help them put down *their* rebels, yet they won't commit resources to aid us? Typical."

Rall shook his head and put the letter down on his desk. "Grant and von Donop are fools." He snorted and shook his head. "That the latter is a fool is hardly a revelation, of course, but I had hoped for better from General Grant. Trenton is *not* sufficiently defensible with only fifteen hundred troops. It's a strategically valuable location, one the colonials may well target. If the rebels *do* attack—"

"May I remind the colonel that our engineers have drawn up plans to physically fortify the town?"

"You may *not* remind me, Colonel," Rall said tartly. "I have already rejected those plans, and I'm not in the habit of repeating myself."

Bowing his head in a gesture that approached respectful, Brethauer said, "Of course, Colonel, my apologies. Will that be all?"

"Yes, Colonel, dismissed."

Brethauer clicked his heels, bowed, and departed the office.

Which was good, as the second communiqué was not for Brethauer's eyes and ears. No, this was a burden that Rall had to bear on his own.

Tonight was a full moon, which meant that tonight he had to perform the ritual that would bring Abaddon's power into the world.

Moloch's instructions were as final as those of von Donop, and the consequences for disobeying them were far greater. Though ironically, Moloch orders served to, in a way, fulfill the request that von Donop and Grant had rejected, for the witch who would be infused with Abaddon's fury would prove to be a valuable ally to the cause, once Rall performed the ritual.

He had already instructed his men not to exceed a single celebratory drink on this Christmas night. Everyone had to be sober if the ritual was to be performed properly. Even though they weren't to participate directly, he needed their life force to help power the spell.

As the full moon rose, Rall opened a bottle of brandy so he could follow his own orders, and have one drink in celebration of the birth of Christ. The irony of his toast to the son of God preceding his bringing a tool of Satan into the world was not lost on him.

After finishing his snifter of brandy, he retired to the sitting room and removed the area rug. Retrieving a piece of chalk from the drawer of his desk, he knelt down and painstakingly drew a sigil on the wooden floor.

In truth, he could have performed the ritual a month ago on the previous full moon, but he had not yet received explicit instructions from Moloch.

His father had tried to anticipate Moloch's wants and needs absent direct instruction. Joachim Rall did not live long enough to make that mistake a second time.

When the sigil was complete, Rall got to his feet

and called out to his adjutant, a very young lieutenant named Piel, who entered and stood at attention. "Sir?"

"Bring Fraulein Serilda in, please."

"Sir!" He hesitated.

"What is it, Lieutenant?" Rall asked impatiently.

"We've received a message from one of the informants, sir." Piel held out a slip of paper.

Rall's rebuke died on his lips. His men had standing orders from the British Crown to always take messages from loyalists who served as informants. But no message was more important than the ritual that he had to perform this night, so he took the slip of paper from Piel, nodded his head, said, "Dismissed, Lieutenant," and shoved the message into his waistcoat pocket.

A few moments later, the door opened again and the woman walked in. She wore a thick black wool cloak, no doubt to protect her from the cold winter weather.

She didn't look like much, this Fraulein Serilda. The woman, who apparently led a coven of witches, had arrived two months earlier, and had spent her entire tenure in Trenton living in a boardinghouse, taking meals at odd hours so she would not have to interact with the other boarders. From what Rall had been told, the other boarders preferred it that way.

The fraulein had not left the boardinghouse, and indeed this was Rall's first time seeing her in person. They had communicated solely by messenger these past eight weeks. What he saw now was an unassuming woman of normal height and build. She threw back the hood of her cloak upon entering Rall's office, revealing herself to have brown hair tied up in a style that he saw every day back home in Stralsund.

"You are not what I expected, Fraulein."

Her eyes, though: they stood out. A deep black, he could get lost in those obsidian pools. Those eyes fixed him now with a penetrating gaze that actually made him take a step back, and he swore his heart skipped a beat.

She spoke with a honeyed voice, and spoke with the accent that was common to the Gypsies of Rall's native land. "Do you doubt our master?"

"Never." Rall said the word emphatically. "Shall we begin?"

"Of course." Serilda removed her cloak, revealing herself to be wearing a simple white shift, with apparently nothing under it.

Rall immediately averted his eyes.

"Do not be a fool," she said with contempt as she pulled the shift over her head, revealing her naked body to him whether he wanted to see it or not. "And do not let false morality interfere with the great work we do." She pulled off each of her boots, revealing bare feet.

"There is nothing foolish about—"

She walked right up to him, forcing him to observe her nakedness directly. "Your priests tell you that the human body is unclean and must remain covered." She smiled nastily. "Those same priests tell you that if you believe in their absurd deity you will live blessed lives. But we both know that they are wrong about that, do we not?"

"Of course," Rall said tightly.

"Then why believe them about this?" She smiled. "Perhaps I should have you strip off your clothes as well."

"That is not necessary for the ritual." Rall knew that the spell would have a transformative effect on Serilda. Her clothing might interfere with that. For him, however, there was no reason to disrobe, and several reasons not to, the chill in the air being primary among them.

With a derisive laugh, she turned on her bare heels and walked to the center of the sigil that was written on the floor.

"Shall we begin?"

Rall let out a long breath. Serilda spoke the truth, of course. He had violated every other tenet of faith that he was raised with back home in Hesse, so why be bound by the nudity taboo?

He held out his hands and began chanting the spell. The language was one that hadn't been spoken on earth with any regularity for millennia, though his father told him once that there were creatures who spoke it conversationally before they were banished to the nether-realms of hell.

The tongue was guttural, even by the standards of the German Rall usually spoke. He wasn't sure what the words meant, though in general he knew that they were terms of summoning.

When he was done, he knew that Serilda would be consumed with dark power that would then be unleashed on the enemies of Moloch. And woe to the foolish rebels who stood in her path.

As he recited the spell, though, he grew frustrated. Nothing was happening. He spoke the nonsense words, Serilda stood in the center of the sigil, and yet nothing changed.

But then he got to the last word of the spell and the furniture started to shake, the glasses on the sideboard began to rattle, and a hot, fetid wind swirled within the sitting room.

Serilda held up her hands. "Come to me, Abaddon! Join your power to mine that we may bring glorious chaos into this world that imprisoned you! Your will be done!"

Another gust of hot wind that smelled like the breath of a rabid dog shoved into Rall's chest, and he stumbled backward. Regaining his footing, he saw Serilda's skin darken and thicken, turning into something that looked like leather. Her black eyes now glowed yellow, her fingers curled into claws, her teeth sharpened into fangs. The strands of her brown hair slowly transmogrified into serpents, reminding Rall of a portrait of Medusa he once saw back home on a Greek vase.

Her arms still upraised, she cackled a mad laugh that echoed throughout the sitting room and chilled Rall to his very bones.

And then there was a flash of light, and Rall felt the heat of a hellish flame bake his face. He held up his arms to shield his eyes from the glow, and suddenly he wished he *had* disrobed, as sweat beaded on his brow and he felt so hot in his long red wool coat that it was as if he'd been transported back to Hesse at the height of midsummer.

It might have been a moment later, it might have been hours, Rall couldn't tell, but when he finally lowered his arms, the light and the heat were gone. He once again felt the winter chill that even the stone of the house and the fireplace couldn't keep at bay.

Of Serilda, there was no sign. All he heard were the echoes of her laughter.

Turning to look to the window, he saw that it was already morning. The ritual felt as if it were but the work of a few minutes, but hours had passed.

Piel ran into the sitting room unbidden and cried, "The rebels have taken the main streets of the town!"

Again Rall was denied a proper rebuke of Piel. "What do you mean?"

"The rebels' general, the man Washington, he has come across Baron de la Warr's river in the night and attacked the Pennington Road outpost after dawn!"

Rall stared at his adjutant for a moment, then shook his head. "Have the regiment form up at the lower end of King Street. Washington and that collection of untrained merchants he calls an army will not take Trenton this day!"

He reached into his waistcoat pocket and finally read the note Piel had given him earlier. With a rueful shake of his head, he saw that it was a warning that Washington's forces would arrive in Trenton imminently.

THE COLD AIR searing his lungs as he rode his white horse, General George Washington led his troops into Trenton. They had faced even less resistance than expected. He had hoped to gain the element of surprise with a predawn attack, but the icy river proved more difficult to pass than he'd hoped. Instead of arriving on the New Jersey side of de la Warr's river at midnight, they didn't arrive until three o'clock, and Generals Cadwallader and Ewing were unable to join them due to the inclement weather.

Under other circumstances, he might have waited until the generals could join him, but he had no time to lose. He *had* to take Trenton. It wasn't just for the reason he gave to the Continental Congress. It was true that, after being expelled from New York, the Continental Army desperately needed a victory before the new year and the enlistments ended.

But salvaging the morale of his troops was sadly

secondary to the reason why he had chosen Trenton as his target after his retreat from Fort Lee: he had to prevent the Hessian Rall from summoning Abaddon. The night of the full moon would be the ideal time for Abaddon's power to be joined with a person, resulting in a half-human creature of enormous power, and enormous evil. According to the intelligence he'd received, the human in question was a witch named Serilda, who ruled over a coven.

When he rode into Trenton the morning of St. Stephen's Day, he knew he was too late. The smell of burning sulfur was one he knew well as the residue of sorcery. Abaddon had already been summoned.

The Hessians who had held Trenton were retreating. Washington saw a man on a horse riding away from him. The man wore the insignia of a lieutenant colonel, and he deduced that this must be Johann Rall, who was one of Moloch's thralls, just as his father had been. Washington took aim with his musket and fired at Rall. The ball struck the enemy, but his horse continued down the thoroughfare away from Washington. He was one of many Hessians running away, and soon Rall's form was lost to his sight.

Quietly he muttered an oath: "May you not live to see the chaos you have unleashed today, Hessian."

Tugging on the reins of his own horse, Washington continued to lead his troops to a victory that was not nearly so great as he had hoped.

FOUR

Sleepy Hollow, New York

JANUARY 2014

THE ISSUE FOR Abbie Mills was always what to order.

In the squad room, it had always been easy. After years of arguments and pissing and moaning every time people had to work late, or there was a big lunch order because everyone was in the office because of paperwork or whatever other reason, Corbin had set up a system. If the cops in HQ wanted to do a big takeout order, where they ordered from depended on the day of the week. Monday and Thursday was pizza, Tuesday and Friday was deli, Wednesday and Saturday was Chinese, and Sunday was Japanese, which was more expensive, but if they were working Sunday, everyone was getting time-and-a-half anyhow, so they could afford it.

One of the things Abbie admired about Captain Irving was that he kept to the "takeout calendar."

Unfortunately, working with Crane had made it kind of difficult to keep to it.

The biggest stumbling block was the food itself. Crane had never had any manner of Asian cuisine in his life, and pizza as modern Americans knew it didn't really exist in Crane's time. The deli provided the only food he even came close to recognizing.

Eventually, he came around to pizza and Chinese, though it usually was accompanied by a Crane Pompous Rant (patent pending).

Tonight, after finding precious little online and even less in Corbin's files on the subject of the Congressional Cross, Mills decided to order a pizza for the simple reason that it was Thursday and they both were hungry.

"You are aware," Crane said after she got off the phone with Salvatore's, "that this bastardized derivation of Greek flatbread only *exists* because of European expansion to this hemisphere. The tomato derives from the Andes Mountains region and was exported to Europe."

Abbie grinned. "Says the man who's never had white pizza."

"Be that as it may, I am boggled by the claim that this is Italian cuisine. I have dined in the region, and there was nothing at all akin to this pizza. As I said, it is far more of a Greek dish."

"Then what could be more in keeping with the spirit of the United States? An Italian variation on a Greek dish made with a South American vegetable by Russian immigrants, delivered to a black woman."

That got Crane to frown. "'Salvatore' does not strike me as a name of Slavic origin."

"It isn't, but he didn't think people would go to a pizza place called Vladimir's."

Crane actually smiled at that, and took a short bow. "I concede the point, Lieutenant." As always, he pronounced her rank like "left tenant," which she had thought pretentious at first, but now had come to really enjoy the sound of.

The door to the armory opened and the captain walked in, holding a large pizza box. "Must be Thursday," he said dryly.

Staring at Irving in surprise, Crane said, "I was unaware, Captain, that you had taken on additional employment delivering foodstuffs."

Abbie chuckled. "Yeah, I didn't think the budget cuts were *that* bad."

"You two are hilarious." Irving put the pizza down on the table next to Abbie's laptop, which she quickly closed. "What's the latest from the wacky world of Moloch and his demonic orchestra? Oh, and you owe me fifteen bucks for the pizza."

Grabbing for her purse, Abbie pulled out a ten and a five and handed them over to Irving. Meanwhile, Crane filled him in on the vision from his wife.

"Wait—*what* was the medal called that you got?"

"I didn't 'get' it," Crane said tartly. "I was merely

awarded it. Had I actually 'gotten' it, I might be more able to fulfill whatever purpose Katrina had in mind with her warning."

Abbie closed her eyes and sighed. She respected Crane a great deal, and he'd become more than a friend over these past few months of craziness, but there were times when she really wanted to just haul off and belt him in the mouth. As she opened the box to the lovely aroma of tomato sauce and melted mozzarella, she actually answered the captain's question: "The Congressional Cross."

"Was it one of ten that were issued by the Continental Congress?"

"Yes." Crane sounded surprised. "Are you aware of them? We've had a difficult time locating specifics, and I'm afraid that I was not present when my own medal was awarded. I was given a certificate via messenger informing me that the Congress had favored me with the award."

"I am aware of them, but only just today."

The captain then told them about his trip to the Metropolitan Museum of Art with his daughter. Abbie was grateful for the independent confirmation that Willett and that asshole van Brunt had received crosses, though she would've preferred that Irving had learned who else had them.

"I don't like this," Irving said. "The same *day* that your mostly dead wife tells you to find your medal, I find out that two of them are missing from their display case."

Abbie frowned. "You don't think they're out for cleaning?"

"I did until five minutes ago."

Crane turned to Abbie with a raised eyebrow. "Coincidence seems to be the order of the day with us, Lieutenant."

Irving shook his head. "I don't believe in coincidence."

"I do," Abbie said. "Coincidences happen all the time. I haven't gone a week on the job without seeing all kinds of coincidences. But I don't *trust* coincidences."

Crane walked over to the pizza box to retrieve a slice. Abbie was pleased to see that this was his first time picking up a slice without losing any cheese off the top, nor having long strings of mozzarella tethering his slice to the rest of the pie. It was that kind of little adjustment that had impressed Abbie about Crane more than the bigger changes he'd gone through to fit into life in modern times. His ability to learn quickly was probably the main thing keeping him alive.

Abbie just hoped that she could keep up with him on that score. While Crane had centuries to catch up on, Abbie had plenty of her own adjustments to deal with.

After taking a bite of pizza, Crane said, "In my own experiences, coincidences have been harbingers of doom." The words were solemn, though the effect was muted by the tomato sauce that got caught in his beard. Abbie seriously considered not telling him about it just to see how long he'd go with sauce on his face, but then Crane himself wiped it away with one of the paper napkins they kept on the table. Abbie had to admit to being disappointed.

"Crane, no offense, but your *presence* is a harbinger of doom." Irving reached into his pocket to pull out his smartphone. "As it happens, the insurance investigator who handles the Met is my former partner."

Abbie blinked. "Really?"

Irving shrugged. "Most insurance investigators are former law enforcement. Bethany Nugent and I went to the academy together, and we both humped the same radio car for a year. She got her twenty, and now she's in insurance. I'll give her a call."

While Irving searched through his phone's address book for the number, Crane gave Abbie one of those looks that she met with a due sense of anticipation and dread. "I believe I have ascertained the meaning of 'radio car,' but I'm not sure of the meaning of the verb 'to hump' in this particular sentence. Also, she received her twenty what, exactly?"

Abbie hesitated. She had a hard enough time explaining regular slang to Crane—explaining cop slang meant going down a road she wasn't entirely sure she'd find her way home from. *Got her twenty* referred to her being on the job for two decades, thus vesting her pension, but she didn't relish the notion of explaining *humped a radio car.*

Irving saved her by putting his phone on speaker and placing it on the table next to the pizza box, the tinny sound of a ringing phone coming from the tiny speakers.

"Sonofabitch," said a sandpapery female voice without fanfare. "I was just thinking that the only way my day could get worse was if I heard from my old partner."

His grin a mile wide, Irving replied, "Well, I'm used to hearing your voice in my nightmares, so I may as well hear it on my phone, too."

Crane was giving Abbie a concerned look, but she just held up a hand and mouthed the words *it's okay*.

"You still working in the 'burbs?"

"Yeah, Sleepy Hollow."

"You *do* remember that Westchester County is where they send the cops who can't cut it in NYPD?"

"Yeah, and the ones who can't cut it in Westchester become insurance investigators."

Nugent's laughter echoed from Irving's phone. "Touché. All right, you may have nothing better to do in Sleeping Halo, but some of us *work* for a living, so let's get to why you called me. Crap, I didn't forget your birthday again, did I?"

"No, this is actually a business call. I've got you on speaker with one of my officers, Abbie Mills, and a consultant we've got in from England, Ichabod Crane."

Now Nugent's tone changed. The time for bantering with an ex-partner had passed and it was down to business. "What's going on?"

"I was down at the Met with Macey yesterday."

Another tone shift, this to friendly concern. "How's she doing?"

"Just fine. She's getting ready for her SATs."

Abbie stared at her captain. The first sentence was an obvious lie, but the second was the declaration of a proud father. She didn't get to see that side of Irving very often, and she had to admit to liking the look of pride on his face.

"Oh c'mon, she can't possibly be old enough to take the SATs. Her ninth-birthday party at Serendipity was only last year."

Irving snorted. "You wish. Yeah, I remember the day she was born like it was last week. Come to think of it, I remember it better than last week."

"You had a really crappy Christmas, too, huh?"

Irving looked over at Abbie and Crane. "My whole life has been pretty crappy, honestly. Anyhow, the reason I called was that Macey and I were looking at an exhibit that was supposed to have two medals in the American Wing—the Congressional Crosses that were awarded to Marinus Willett and Abraham van Brunt. Thing is, we've got a lead from one of our CIs that somebody might be targeting those crosses."

"How—oh, right, suburbs. 'Course you got CIs

who can give you intel on art heists. Probably know which wineries are being targeted, too, right?"

Abbie recognized the stalling tactic. "Ms. Nugent, this is Lieutenant Mills. Captain Irving told us that the crosses were out for cleaning, but I'm guessing by your use of the term 'art heist' that the cleaning thing is just for the general public?"

"Score one for the suburban cop. Look, Frank, I can't have this getting out. We've kept the press, NYPD, and FBI out of it, but—"

That got Abbie's eyes to go wide. "You didn't report it?"

"Not *yet*—we think it was someone inside, and we want to try to take care of it internally first. If that doesn't pan out, I'll go down to the one-nine myself and fill out the report."

Crane gave Abbie another of his patented confused looks, and he mouthed, *one nine?*

Abbie held up a hand to indicate that she'd explain later that Nugent was referring to the 19th Precinct of the NYPD, which included the Metropolitan in its domain. She did that a lot. . . .

"Don't worry, Beth, Lieutenant Mills and Mr. Crane are part of a classified task force. They aren't gonna be talking to *anybody* about any of this." Irving punctuated that with a look at each of them. Crane looked nonplussed, but Abbie just gave the captain her *are you serious?* look.

"All right," Nugent said, "let me finish up our investigation here. Give me two days, and if I haven't nailed anything down, I'll take a drive up the Saw Mill Parkway, and we'll compare notes."

"Sounds like a plan. Thanks, Beth."

"Miss Nugent, this is Ichabod Crane."

Abbie winced. It was always dangerous when Crane started talking to people who weren't part of the craziness.

"Yeah, the consultant. Nice accent."

"Er, thank you. I have a query regarding the crosses. By what means did they come into your museum's possession?"

"Both of them were gifted to the museum about a hundred years ago by descendants of the original owners. It was van Brunt's grand-nephew and Willett's great-grandson or some such. I could look it up if you want."

"No need. My thanks."

Irving reached for the phone. "Thanks again, Beth. We'll talk soon."

"You bet. And give that kid of yours a kiss on the head from her old aunt Beth, 'kay?"

Irving smiled. "Will do. Take care." He ended the call.

Crane turned his confused look on Irving. "In the early stages of your conversation, I feared that this Miss Nugent was a great enemy of yours."

Abbie was startled by Irving laughing in response to that. Irving hardly even smiled, much less laughed, to the point where she wouldn't be able to swear on a Bible that Irving had teeth.

"Yeah," the captain said, "I can see why you'd think that."

"I imagine that your verbal japes derive from the time you spent humping with your radio car?"

Now it was Abbie's turn to laugh. "Great, now we've got him mangling cop slang. We're doomed."

FIVE

TARRYTOWN, NEW YORK

JANUARY 2014

CAROLYN TOLLEY HAD no idea how her life had been reduced to working as a security guard in the Cortlandt Museum in Tarrytown.

It seemed like it was just yesterday that she was working a high-paying job at a money management firm on Hudson Street, with a beautiful apartment on the Upper West Side, the best husband in the world, and a wonderful son.

With Jamal doing well in high school and about to go off to college, she and Greg had been looking into houses in Tarrytown, Sleepy Hollow, Hastings-on-Hudson, and other locations in the Lower Hudson Valley. They'd even put a down payment on a place in Hastings.

But then Greg got laid off. And then his unemployment ran out without any job prospects. A lot of close calls, but nothing solid. The bank withdrew the approval of their mortgage because of Greg's unemployment.

And then everything happened at once. Greg came back from what he said was a job interview completely drunk and assaulted her badly enough to send her to the hospital. After she filed a police report, she learned that he'd blown through their savings on alcohol and had been out drinking all the times he was supposedly on interviews or at job fairs.

He used the last of the savings on bail, and then proceeded to drive their car into a truck that was in the middle of the intersection of Columbus Avenue and West 100th Street. The very next day, Jamal was arrested for drug possession. He did a deal with the district attorney to give up his supplier in exchange for probation, but then the dealer in question got someone to shoot Jamal in the back of the head.

The day after that, she was informed that her boss had fled to the Bahamas with all the firm's money, just barely ahead of an SEC investigation that would likely have shut the place down anyhow.

All of that happened while Carolyn was in a bed in St. Luke's–Roosevelt Hospital recovering from the broken arm, broken leg, and facial contusions her late husband had given her.

She had an even harder time finding work than Greg had, as her association with the disgraced firm was a scarlet letter on her résumé. Nobody would even give her an interview at her level, and every time she applied for a lesser job, she was rejected for being overqualified. "You'll be bored and leave in a month."

Carolyn kept telling them that she was willing to be bored if she could make rent.

Eventually, she had to give up the place on Ninety-Seventh Street and take a crappy apartment in Sleepy Hollow. She got a job working night security at the museum, one of three guards who kept an eye on the valuables while the place was closed.

She'd found it ironic that she got a job as a security guard, when she'd been too unobservant to notice that her husband was a drunk, her son was a drug addict, and her boss was a thief.

Right now, she sat glancing over the security camera footage of all the galleries. Next to her was her partner at the front desk, Kyle Means. In front of her was the paperback novel that she'd finished halfway through the shift, and she had neglected to bring a second one.

Kyle was reading off a tablet, which gave Carolyn a pang of jealousy. She'd had a Kindle, but the screen died, and she couldn't afford to replace it. Not that she could afford to buy books anymore, either—the one she'd finished came from the Warner Library on North Broadway—but she still missed having the damn thing. Not to mention a television, an iPod, a smartphone . . . All of them had died, and the only one she replaced was the phone, but she now had a flip phone that couldn't even send text messages.

Her radio squawked. "Hey, Carolina, where you at? Shoulda come by me on your walk-through by now?"

Carolyn had long since given up correcting Pedro Gomez's mispronunciation of her name. She'd met him at the dojo in Hastings that she went to for the first month after moving here, before she could no longer afford the tuition. It was affiliated with the one on the Upper West Side that she used to attend when she lived there. He'd been the one to tell her about this job. She figured that was worth his misremembering her first name.

She grabbed the radio to reply to the third guard, whose job it was to guard the loading dock. Like the front door she and Kyle sat near, it was gated and locked. "My knee's acting up, Pedro, I'd just as soon not bother with the walk-through. It's not like we *need* to do it since the cameras cover everything. Hell, they don't need three of us here, either. We can just tell Myra I did it, okay?"

"That's dishonest, Carolina. I got too much to confess on Sunday, I no wanna add lying to that."

Looking over at Kyle, she asked, "Meanie?"

He didn't even look up from his tablet. "I did the last walk-through, and I *have* to finish this chapter for class tomorrow." Then he did look up. "Besides, I asked you to stop calling me that."

Carolyn chuckled. She couldn't help it. Kyle was the nicest person she'd ever met, and so she couldn't resist the nickname. "Cut me some slack, Meanie, I don't get much by way of amusement these days." With a sigh, she pulled herself to her feet, wincing as her knee made several unfortunate noises that were very much like what Rice Krispies sounded like after you poured in the milk.

Kyle winced. "Oooh, that sounds bad."

"Yeah, well, that's what happens when you lose your health coverage before you get referred to do physical therapy." She grabbed the radio. "All right, Pedro, I'll do it, but when I get to the loading dock, you gotta promise to tell me some of the things you *are* confessing Sunday."

"I'll tell you *one* thing, Carolina."

"Deal." Carolyn put the radio in its holster and started gingerly walking through the lobby toward the first of the gallery rooms she had to eyeball. It wasn't quite a limp, but it wasn't a comfortable gait, either. Thanks to the Affordable Care Act, she finally had health coverage again starting New Year's Day, and it hadn't come a moment too soon. She'd made an appointment with a local doctor to look over her leg for next Wednesday. The arm seemed to have healed just fine, but the leg had never been right since she checked out of St. Luke's.

She entered the Yellow Room—all the galleries were named after the color scheme of the paint job—which had a bunch of portraits of people who were long dead and who probably were famous for something. Carolyn had never had any interest in art, so the contents of the building were meaningless to her. If the museum was full of shoes, she might have been interested.

Carolyn really missed shoe shopping.

Shaking her head at her own shallowness, she moved on to the Green Room, which had landscapes. Dead drunk husband, dead junkie son, and all she could lament was that she couldn't go shoe shopping anymore because she was stuck in a minimum-wage job in a museum full of stuff she didn't give a damn about.

The Cortlandts were one of the rich families that moved up to the Lower Hudson Valley in the nineteenth century. While they weren't as famous—or as pervasive—as the Rockefellers, they did plenty, including opening this museum, which was now run by the Cortlandt Trust, in the person of a spectacularly annoying married couple. The husband, Daniel Kapsis, handled the money, while his wife, Myra, took care of personnel. She was the one who insisted on the walk-throughs, even though the security cameras that covered every room had normal light and also infrared capability. The simple fact was that the cameras just needed someone to keep an eye on them. They didn't need three sets of eyes doing the job less well than the cameras when the museum wasn't even open. Sure, when there were people in the building, having actual security guards standing around looking vaguely intimidating was useful, but after hours? It was a waste.

Not that she was going to complain. God knew she needed the job to survive, just as Kyle needed it to pay for Marymount College and Pedro needed it to support him, his elderly mother, his niece, and his numerous girlfriends. She was hoping that the latter would be the subject of his shared confession when she got to the loading bay.

The closest she came to anything interesting was in the Blue Room, which had the decorative arts. She couldn't give a damn about paintings or sculptures, but she always thought it was cool to see what kind of things people had around the house.

When the museum was closed, the large fluorescent ceiling lights were turned off, but the small lamps that illuminated the artwork were left on. However, when she went into the Blue Room, those lights were all out.

She grabbed her radio with one hand and reached for her flashlight with the other. "Hey, Meanie, we lose power in the Blue Room?"

Kyle's tinny voice sounded over the radio speaker a moment later. "Nope, lights are on and I see you in the doorway. Why, what's up?"

Carolyn blinked. She one-handedly fumbled

with her flashlight and switched it on—but the light that came from it only made it about a quarter inch from the bulb before it was swallowed by darkness. "It's pitch black in here."

"I'm not seeing it, Carolyn."

She slowly moved farther into the room, but the flashlight continued to be useless.

Then the temperature just dropped. Carolyn shivered from the freezing cold. "What the hell? You put the AC on, Meanie?"

"It's *January*, Carolyn; the AC *can't* be turned on until the first of May."

"Right." Carolyn had actually forgotten that—but then, she hadn't started the job until the late fall, so she hadn't paid all that much attention to what the air-conditioning was supposed to do. "So what the hell's going—"

Go away!

Before she even realized that she'd done it, Carolyn found herself running back to the Green Room. The voice had sounded *in her head*.

Violently shaking her head back and forth as if to dislodge the voice that had appeared there, Carolyn yelled into her radio. "Meanie, hit the alarm *right now*, there's someone in the Blue Room!"

"Carolyn, I'm not seeing anything, except you running out of the room for no good reason. What's going on down there?"

Pedro said, "I'll come check it out."

"Look, I know it sounds crazy!" Carolyn realized she was shouting, and took a quick breath to calm herself down. "I heard someone yell at me to go away."

Kyle was insistent. "Carolyn, I don't see anything in the—"

After Kyle's pause went on for two seconds, Carolyn prompted him. "Meanie, what's going on?"

"I—This is crazy. One of the display cases is opening up by itself."

Pedro's voice then came again. "Carolina, I'm at the far entrance. I don't see nothing, just black."

Carolyn found herself unable to make her creaky legs move herself back toward the Blue Room.

"This is crazy," Kyle was saying in an ever-more-hysterical tone. "I see the room perfectly clearly—Pedro, I see you standing in the doorway—but there's nobody there, but the case is opening! Oh, hell, now the cross is floating!"

"Cross?" Carolyn asked. If she remembered right, it was a cross that was awarded to somebody back during the American Revolution—or maybe it was the French and Indian War. Half the stuff in here related to one of those wars, and Carolyn couldn't keep it straight. She was less interested in history than she was in art.

"I'm goin' in," Pedro said. "Whoever is in here, do not move! The police have been called and—*auuuuuuuugh*!"

The sudden scream startled Carolyn out of her

stupor, and she ran for the door to the Blue Room—immediately stumbling and falling to the floor. Running wasn't really in her repertoire these days. The bitter taste of adrenaline welled up in her throat as she clambered to her feet, wondering what could have caused Pedro to emit such a bloodcurdling scream.

Kyle was now yelling over the radio. "Pedro? Pedro, what happened? Carolyn, the cameras are all dead, I can't see anything!"

"Did you call the cops?"

"Just sounded the alarm."

"Took you long enough." Carolyn got to her feet and went into the Blue Room.

The darkness had lifted, and now the exhibits were all again illuminated by the small lamps. All the exhibits were in place, except for the cross, which was missing, its case opened wide.

Carolyn barely noticed those things, though, because of what she saw on the floor.

All the parts of Pedro's body were lying on the marble floor, but they weren't all connected to each other anymore. His head was by one display case, his torso was in the center of the floor, each arm was on either side of the room, and his legs were on top of another display case.

There was surprisingly little blood, though despite having lost both her husband and son in the past year, her experiences with dead bodies were limited.

She wasn't sure why she wasn't screaming. She also wasn't sure why she wasn't moving or yelling into the radio or running away like a sensible person or really doing much of *anything* except just *staring* at Pedro's head.

It just didn't make any sense. Greg had already established himself as a drunk when he drove into the truck. Jamal had already established himself as a junkie when he got shot by a drug dealer. But Pedro was just alive a few seconds ago. It made no sense that he was dead now.

Another second or two passed before she realized that the cross was floating in midair.

Then the room grew dark again. On the one hand, Carolyn was relieved, as she no longer could see Pedro's body.

But then the cold came back, and then she felt— well, *something* in the room, like the darkness had form and substance.

That was impossible, of course, but nevertheless she could *feel* the darkness closing in on her.

Specifically, closing in on her neck. She couldn't breathe, all of a sudden, as something tightened around her throat. Carolyn tried to swallow, tried to inhale, to exhale, *something*, but she couldn't.

Kyle's voice was screaming over the radio. "Will someone please tell me what the *hell* is going on?"

It was the last thing Carolyn heard. She had finally worked up the will to scream when she felt something cold and awful begin to slice through her neck.

ABBIE MILLS HAD only just entered her bedroom when her phone buzzed. They had decided to call it a night at the armory. She had only just dropped Crane off at Corbin's old cabin, and she really wanted a good night's sleep.

"I swear, Crane, if this is you . . ." She trailed off when the display showed an unfamiliar 914 area code number.

Hitting the talk button on her phone's screen, she put it to her ear. "Mills."

"Lieutenant Mills? This is Officer Wang. I'm sorry, did I wake you?"

"That would've happened if you called two minutes later."

"I'm sorry, ma'am, but my sergeant said you were the one to call whenever some Mulder-and-Scully stuff happens."

Rubbing the bridge of her nose between her thumb and forefinger, Abbie asked, "What happened?"

"It's at the Cortlandt Museum in Tarrytown. It's, ah—it's really kinda gross. We've got three bodies that aren't just dead, they've been ripped to pieces."

By this point, Abbie had left her bedroom and gone back to the kitchen, where she'd unceremoniously tossed her leather jacket on one of the chairs. "I'll be there as fast as I can. And tell your sergeant to update his TV references."

Wang sounded contrite. "Yeah, actually, that was me. Had a crush on Gillian Anderson when I was a kid."

"Thanks, Officer Wang. See you soon."

After swinging back by Corbin's cabin to pick up Crane, Abbie drove them to the Cortlandt Museum. Half a dozen blue-and-whites were parked in front of the Victorian-era stone building that had been the Cortlandt family's mansion when they had moved here in the late nineteenth century. Red and blue lights flashed in eye-tearing irregular patterns, illuminating the night sky. Also parked nearby was a van from the Westchester County medical examiner.

As soon as she climbed out of her car, Abbie saw Detective Costa standing by the entrance to the museum and winced.

"What is the matter, Lieutenant?" Crane asked as he exited from the passenger side.

"That's Lisa-Anne Costa. She tends to get territorial about her cases, and she also hates consultants."

"Ah, so she shall welcome the assistance of another detective and a consultant with open arms," Crane said dryly.

Abbie regarded Crane with a smile. "I don't know why, but it makes me think the world's a better place knowing that sarcasm was around in the eighteenth century, too."

Costa caught sight of Abbie and immediately made a beeline for her, her trench coat billowing behind her as she walked through the cold night air.

"The hell *you* doing here, Mills? This is a Tarrytown case."

"I called her, ma'am," came a voice from Abbie's left. She turned to see a short Asian man in uniform. This had to be Officer Wang. "We were told during roll call, if we had any crazy stuff, to call these two."

She pointed an angry finger at Wang. "Your sergeant and I are having *words*." Then Costa turned to Abbie. "Ain't nothin' for you here, Sleepy Hollow. This is a Tarrytown case, and I got this. Go home, get some sleep, you can read about it in the *Journal News* tomorrow, got me?"

Abbie started to reply, but Crane spoke up before she could. She considered talking over him, but she had had enough run-ins with Costa to know that responding would only start a shouting match. Abbie was in a bad enough mood that she might actually enjoy going six rounds with Costa, but that wouldn't do much good for finding out what was going on in the museum. Maybe Crane's Old World charm would succeed where Abbie's New World bitchiness failed.

"Detective Costa, if you would be so kind to at least inform us of what occurred here tonight.

Based on Officer Wang's communication with Lieutenant Mills, it's quite possible that this relates to our own ongoing inquiries that began with the decapitation of Sheriff Corbin, Mr. Ogelvie, and Reverend Knapp. We have no interest in usurping your rightful place in command of *this* investigation, but we do wish to know if it coincides in any way with ours."

Costa just stared at Crane for several seconds, her mouth open and forming an oval.

Finally, she turned to Abbie. "Where'd you dig this one up, Mills?"

Abbie came within a hairsbreadth of saying, "In a cave outside town," but managed to restrain herself.

"All right, look, I wasn't gonna say anything till you reminded me of that triple beheading. 'Cause we got us another one. C'mon in." She turned, her trench coat again billowing.

Crane and Abbie both followed, the former asking the latter, "How does she enable her topcoat to—to *flow* in such a manner?"

Abbie just chuckled.

They ducked under the yellow crime-scene tape across the museum entrance, and then Abbie saw the first of the three bodies—all five parts of it. His head had rolled into a corner, and was staring upward, with the right arm and left leg on top of the security desk. The other limbs were in the opposite corner from the head, with the torso lying right in the middle of the floor.

"There's not enough blood." Abbie said the words before she even realized why she spoke them aloud.

"Good work, Detective," Costa said snarkily. "This was Kyle Means, one of the three security guards that the Cortlandt Trust had on the payroll. And you're right, you slice up a body like this, there should be a helluva lot more blood. And the ME confirmed that the wounds were *not* cauterized, so I got no damn clue."

She then led Abbie and Crane through two gallery rooms before they reached a room containing two similar sets of body parts. One torso was female, the other male, and Abbie saw the heads of an African-American woman and a Latino man. There was the same lack of blood.

Crane said, "I observe, Detective, that there are no noticeable gaps in the displays. It does not appear that any of the treasures in this museum were removed."

"Almost." Costa pointed at one display case, which was open.

Peering into it, Abbie saw that the red felt of the display case had a cross-shaped spot that was lighter than the rest of the visible felt, plus there was a placard under it.

Then she read the placard. "Sonofabitch."

"What is it, Lieutenant?" Crane asked.

In response, Abbie just pointed at the placard.

Crane bent over to read it aloud. "'This Independence Cross was crafted by the French silversmith Gaston Mercier. It is one of ten Mercier created, which were issued to soldiers of the American Revolutionary War who showed special valor in the defense of freedom against the tyranny of the British crown. The cross, which was also known as the Congressional Cross due to its being issued by the Second Continental Congress'"—at that point, Crane shot Abbie a look—"'was awarded to Ezekiel Cortlandt in 1775, and was issued with the other nine in 1785 after they were completed.' Fascinating."

Costa was frowning. "Fascinating, how, exactly?"

"Can't say yet," Abbie said quickly before Crane said something he shouldn't. "It might be related to our case. It might not. We'll keep you posted."

"Fine." Costa didn't seem happy with that answer, but she didn't seem unhappy with it, either, which suited Abbie fine. She started leading the pair of them toward the door. "Let's go. You've seen what you gotta see, now it's time to go."

As they went through the other galleries, Abbie asked, "You get anything from the security footage?"

"Nah, it was deleted. Whoever did this was a pro." Costa snorted. "A professional *what* I ain't sure, but they thought to erase the footage. Not just the cameras, the computers they feed to are *com-*

pletely wiped. Hopin' our nerd squad can reconstruct some of it."

As soon as they got to the front door, Costa said, "*See* ya," and turned back on her heel, allowing her coat to billow one last time.

"That *is* impressive," Crane said admiringly as she retreated back into the museum.

Abbie rolled her eyes and ducked under the tape.

As soon as she did, an older man approached her. She squinted at him, as he looked like he'd thrown the suit on in a hurry—but the suit in question cost more than Abbie made in a month.

"Excuse me, are you the detective in charge? I need to know what the hell's going on in there."

"And you are?"

"My name is Daniel Kapsis, my wife and I are in charge of the Cortlandt Trust, and we *demand* to know what's going on!"

Abbie gave Kapsis her best screw-you smile, one perfected over years of dealing with abusive citizens who just loved getting into a cop's face. "I'm sorry, Mr. Kapsis, I'm afraid I'm *not* the detective in charge. You want to talk to Detective Lisa-Anne Costa. She just went inside, but I'm sure you can grab her, just duck under that yellow tape."

"Excellent. Thank you." Kapsis pushed right past her and ducked under the tape. Two uniforms saw that and chased after him as he went inside.

Crane looked down at Abbie. "You enjoyed that."

"You're damn right. C'mon, let's try to get *some*

sleep. I need a crowbar to keep my eyelids open right now. Don't worry," she added, holding up a hand, "I'm fine to drive. I need to be a lot more tired than this before I can't operate a motor vehicle."

"There *are* livery services that can—"

"I'll get you home," Abbie said tightly. "In the morning, I'll give Jenny a call and we'll dive into the research. We got three dead bodies, so this is a real thing now."

"Not just three corpses, Lieutenant." Crane glanced back at the museum. "Three murders that were committed via supernatural means."

Abbie nodded. "Yeah, no way those bodies were killed by anybody—or anything—normal. The *good* news is that we've got another name for that medal of yours. Maybe we'll get more hits on the Independence Cross than we did on the Congressional Cross."

"And perhaps we may learn what happened to my own cross."

"Yeah." Abbie sighed. "Let's hope so."

SIX

SLEEPY HOLLOW, NEW YORK

JANUARY 2014

"COPS SUCK."

Jennifer Mills burst out with this interjection after searching through her third file cabinet trying to find the copy of *Tobin's Spirit Guide*.

Everyone else in the room—her sister Abbie, Crane, and Captain Irving—all looked up from what they were doing. Crane was surprised; Abbie just smiled.

But the captain got that just-ate-a-sour-lemon look he always seemed to get around Jenny. "What the hell's *that* supposed to mean?"

"Just what I said." She slammed a cabinet drawer shut. "Corbin had all this stuff meticulously organized. It was indexed, filed, subfiled, cross-referenced—made the Library of Congress look like a recycling bin. You cops come in, take it all away, and just toss it all across the street in this little dungeon of yours. No organization, no cross-referencing, nothing. How exactly are we supposed to save the world if we can't find what we need to save the world with?"

There was a brief pause as everyone just kind of stared at Jenny. It was like she was back in the loony bin again.

Finally the captain spoke again. "Believe me, if I'd known the fate of the world depended on this stuff, we'd have taken better care of it. But all we knew was that Corbin had a whole lot of useless crap in his office and we needed to clear space."

They'd spent the better part of the day going over Corbin's files and searching online, trying to find out everything they could about the medals that had been stolen, and how it might relate to Crane's vision. Abbie also looked into the places where they knew the medals were displayed, leaving messages and asking for status updates. Irving had had to go off and do his captain thing periodically, so he wasn't contributing as much, but they'd started first thing in the morning, and it was now starting to get dark.

"Anyhow," Abbie said before Jenny could get into it any further with Irving, "why don't we take a break and see where we are?"

"Agreed," Crane said.

Jenny shook her head. "Fine."

Abbie glared at Jenny, who just glared right back.

So Abbie indicated Irving with her head. Jenny just rolled her eyes, and Abbie indicated Irving with her head again. This time Jenny shook her head and folded her arms.

That just got Abbie to sigh, but Jenny didn't care. She was *not* going to apologize to that jerk, and Abbie should've known better.

Jenny had spent so much time loving her sister, so much time hating her, and so much time just not understanding her. Sometimes it was all three at once, and this was one of those times. She appreciated the concern she had, yet she was annoyed that Abbie thought it was something she had to apologize for.

Then again, she was a cop, and so was Irving. Cops, as she had pointed out a few minutes ago, sucked.

"As far as can be determined," Crane said, "there are six of the Congressional Crosses—or Independence Crosses—extant. Of those six, three have gone missing. There is the one belonging to Ezekiel Cortlandt, stolen last night, and the ones belonging to Marinus Willett and Abraham van Brunt, recently stolen from the large museum in New York."

Jenny regarded Crane with a raised eyebrow. "You okay, Crane?"

Crane closed his eyes and sighed. "It is not necessary for you all to be concerned regarding my feelings toward my erstwhile best friend. The van Brunt I knew is dead. The creature we captured, the creature whom I beheaded, is a demon who is using van Brunt's body and his relationship to Katrina to hurt me." He then smiled wryly. "At least, that is what I tell myself to ease the guilt and anger. Regardless, my friendship with van Brunt has no bearing on this particular task we must perform."

"We even know what the task is?" Irving asked. "Right now, all we got is three dead bodies and three stolen medals."

"Three gruesomely dead bodies." Abbie shook her head.

"If *you're* calling it gruesome . . ." Jenny shuddered. She and her sister had seen plenty of sights, together and separately, that pretty much redefined the word *gruesome* in both their lexicons. It wasn't a word either used lightly anymore. Jenny then went on to answer the captain's question. "If there's any significance to these medals, I haven't found it yet. There's no mention of it in any of the texts that Corbin gathered." She shot Irving a look. "At least that I've been able to *find*."

Irving just gave her the sour-lemon look again. "You volunteering to organize it?"

Before Jenny could reply, Abbie snorted.

"What was that?" Jenny asked.

"What was what?" Abbie tried and failed to look all innocent.

"That snort."

"Oh, just remembering what your room always looked like. Organization's not exactly your strong suit. Only neat room you ever lived in was Room 49, and I'm guessing they *made* you keep it tidy."

Jenny folded her arms and gave her a nasty look, but before she could respond to what she viewed as a wholly gratuitous and unfair reference to the room she was assigned to at Tarrytown Psychiatric Hospital, Crane spoke up.

"If we may return to the issue at hand?"

Rolling her eyes, Jenny said, "Fine."

"The other three crosses that we've been able to find are likewise in museums. Lieutenant Mills found one yesterday, belonging to Tench Tilghman. It is normally on display in the District of Columbia, but there is a traveling exhibit about the Society of the Cincinnati, of which Tilghman was a member. It's currently ensconced in the Museum of the City of New York. Another, which was given to Henry Knox, is at Fort Ticonderoga—when did they change the name?"

"Excuse me?" Abbie asked.

"It was Fort Carillon in my day. The *region* was called Ticonderoga, an Iroquois word referring to the two lakes that met there."

"Well, you'll love it," Irving said. "I took the family up there a few years ago, and the fort's been completely restored to what it was like back in the day."

Crane's eyes went wide the way they always did when he found out something new, though usually it led to him bitching and moaning about something. "Has it? I should very much like to see such a thing."

As usual, Abbie kicked the subject back in bounds. "Where's the last one?"

"Conveniently," Crane said, pointing at a local map that was laid out on one of the tables, "it's right here in Sleepy Hollow."

Jenny followed his finger, which pointed at the Whitcombe-Sears Library over on Chestnut Street. "I know the place. Corbin sent me there to do research a few times. It's in an old Episcopal church that got converted about fifty years ago."

"We must protect these locations," Crane said. "They are likely to be targeted next."

"Unless they only need three of 'em." Abbie was always good at pouring cold water on a perfectly good plan.

The captain put his two cents in. "Or our drawn-and-quarterer has the ones that are unaccounted for."

Crane stared at Irving. "'Drawn-and-quarterer'?"

"I'm a police captain," Irving deadpanned. "I can make up words if I want to. So, what's the plan, Stan?"

"My—my name is Ichabod." Now Crane got all befuddled, which resulted in his lost-puppy look. Of Crane's many and varied facial expressions, Jenny found that one to be the most entertaining.

"It's a song quote, Crane," Jenny said. "And cut him some slack, Cap. He's not gonna know Paul Simon."

"Surprised you do." Irving actually chuckled at that.

"I'm *very* complicated," Jenny said in a mock-arrogant tone. "So, we sure these medals are where they're supposed to be?"

Abbie checked her phone. "Just got a text back from one of the docents at Ticonderoga. Knox's Independence Cross is still in its case."

Crane pointed at Abbie's laptop. "The Society of the Cincinnati exhibit has some manner of surveillance machine that allows one to see the exhibit from a distance."

Grinning, Abbie said, "It's called a webcam, and Tilghman's cross is intact, too."

Irving nodded. "And I'd've heard if anybody had broken into Whitcombe-Sears."

"Okay, so we split up." Jenny clapped her hands. Corbin had showed her the value of doing research, but at this point, she'd been sitting on her ass long enough. She was ready to take action. "I can sit on MCNY."

Abbie was shaking her head, but it was Irving who spoke. "Nah, I got the museum. I've got NYPD connections—past and present—that can help me out there."

"Fine, I can take Crane up to Ticonderoga. Can't wait to see the look on his—"

"No." Abbie said the word with a lot more intensity than Jenny thought was at all warranted.

"Excuse me?" Jenny stared at her sister with a

hard expression. She was *not* putting up with her crap on this, and did not want to make this one of the times she hated her sister.

"You'll take Whitcombe-Sears. You already know the place."

Jenny rolled her eyes. "I've been there maybe three times, and the last time was years ago. Why can't I go to Ticonderoga?"

Abbie closed her eyes, then opened them again. "Because it's against the law."

"Say *what*?"

"Part of the terms of your release from Tarrytown Psychiatric into my custody was that you would stay in Westchester County. You can't go down to the city, you can't go across to Jersey, you can't go east to Connecticut, and you can't go upstate. That's the deal, and if you break that deal, it's back to Room 49 you go."

Crane frowned. "I can't imagine that they would assign Miss Jenny the same room when . . ." He trailed off, probably seeing the look on Jenny's face. She was certainly going for majorly pissed-off.

"This *sucks*."

"I agree, but it was the only way to get the judge to sign off on your release."

Jenny stared angrily at her sister, but this time Abbie wasn't giving her a nasty look back. It was a look of apology and of guilt.

Abbie walked up to Jenny and put a hand on her

shoulder. "Look, Jenny, cops may suck—but judges suck more."

Unable to help herself, Jenny burst out with a laugh. "Guess so. All right, fine, I'll head to the library."

"Thanks for understanding."

"Oh, no." Jenny took a step back and shook her head. "This isn't understanding. At best, this is resignation."

"Fair enough." Abbie turned to Crane. "It's four hours to Ticonderoga from here. We hit the road now, we can get a motel room for the night and check the fort out in the morning."

"Very well." Crane nodded.

Abbie then turned to Irving. "I don't suppose I can get the department to pay for the motel?"

Jenny again couldn't help bursting out with a laugh.

For Irving, though, it was just a chuckle. "You want the honest answer or the polite answer?"

Crane frowned. "The polite one, I should think."

"*Hell* no, not in your wildest dreams."

That just deepened Crane's frown. "If you knew the full tenor of my dreams, Captain, you would not make such a statement. And I shudder to think what the honest answer was."

Abbie quickly said, "My credit card can handle it, as long as we stick with a cheap-ass motel. I'm still paying off the movers who had to ship everything *back* when I changed my mind about moving to D.C., plus I lost the security deposit on the apartment down there."

Jenny chuckled. "Always the little things, ain't it, sis?"

Irving nodded. "Yeah, all right. I got some other business in the city to take care of anyhow." He pulled out his cell phone and called someone. After a few rings: "Hey, Beth. Listen, I need you to do me a favor. . . ."

Whatever favor Irving wanted this Beth woman to do for him was lost as the captain left the room.

"Who's Beth?" she asked Abbie.

"His former partner. She's an insurance investigator for the company that insures the Met these days. She's the one that verified that the medals were stolen."

Jenny nodded. "Cool. All right, I'll head over to the library soon, then. I want to check a few more things here."

"We'll hit the road." Abbie looked at Crane. "Let's go."

Crane gave one of his bows. "Happy hunting, Miss Jenny."

"You too, Crane."

Jenny spent the next hour trying and failing to organize Corbin's files. Each time she took a shot at it, she either got distracted by something interesting to read—there was one musty old book that had all kinds of interesting stuff about healing potions and herbs—or got fed up and stopped after only sorting a few things because it was boring.

To her horror, she was going to have to admit that her older sister was right.

Considering she'd been spending the better part of a decade thinking of Abbie as nothing but wrong, this was a bit of a revelation for her.

Putting it out of her mind, she left the armory and headed up to North Broadway and then down to Chestnut Street.

The first time Jenny had set foot in the Whitcombe-Sears Library, it was in the company of Sheriff Corbin.

"This old church is a library?" she had asked the sheriff when he brought her down Chestnut the first time.

Corbin had smiled under his beard. "Hasn't been a church of any kind in fifty years. It was Episcopal, and done in the Federal style—which is why it's made out of brick instead of stonework, and why the inside was boring as hell. Give me a good old-fashioned Gothic church or Catholic cathedral any day."

Jenny had stopped walking and given him a look. "Is this gonna be another lecture? 'Cause if it is, I can go back home *right* now."

Putting a reassuring hand on her back, he guided her forward. "No lecture, I promise. At least not from me."

They had gone inside the large wooden double

doors, which opened with a creak. Inside was a small hallway with a staircase on the left and a wall on the right that had a bulletin board covered with flyers about various happenings and services in the town. In front of them sat a doorway to the larger church area—or, rather, library area—which had a small security gate designed to read the bar codes on books that hadn't been checked out.

Past the gate had been rows of bookcases where pews probably used to be. Looking up, she saw more bookcases up on the balcony where the organ probably was. Up front, in the area where the altar would have been, sat a huge wooden desk.

Corbin had made a beeline for that desk. On top of it had been a pile of books, a computer that was top-of-the-line the year Jenny was born—the fan was making a labored noise—and a wooden box containing call slips and small pencils. On either side there had been two small tables with computers of the same vintage as the antique on the desk, which Jenny had figured to be for the use of the general public.

Said public had been nowhere to be found, as the two of them had been the only patrons present in the library.

Behind the desk had sat a middle-aged man with a beard that was even grayer than Corbin's, and with thinning wispy salt-and-pepper hair, which was tied back in a ponytail.

Without preamble, Corbin had smiled and said

to the man behind the desk, "You know that desk violates the fire code, don't you?"

The librarian—at least, Jenny had assumed he was a librarian, though she never did find out for sure—had just grinned. "So cite me, you old reprobate."

Corbin had put out his hand over the desk, and the librarian shook it enthusiastically. "Good to see you." He had turned to Jenny then. "Jenny Mills, this is Albert Whitcombe-Sears, the proprietor of this august place of learning."

"Thank you, August," Al had said, mispronouncing Corbin's first name with the accent on the second syllable like the adjective Corbin had used to describe the library. Then he had offered her his own hand. "Pleased to meet you, Jenny—but you can call me Al. Just don't call me Betty."

Jenny had returned the handshake, and had also given him a confused look. "Why would I call you Betty?"

Corbin had waved the joke off. "Paul Simon song."

"Who?"

"I'll burn you some CDs. Trust me, you'll be grateful. Anyhow, Al, we need to look up some genealogical stuff going back to the early nineteenth century. Involves a haunting up in Douglas Park."

"You know, this church hadn't been built yet," Whitcombe-Sears had said. "It was all Dutch Reform around here in those days. Wasn't until the railroad that all the rich Protestants started moving up here. Then, suddenly, we had Episcopalians and Presbyterians and the like. Then the auto industry showed up, and it was all poor immigrants, who were almost entirely Catholic, so this place becomes a library."

Jenny had glared at Corbin. "You promised me no lectures."

"No, I promised you no lectures *from me*."

The research they had done that day had been less useful than Corbin had hoped, though they had taken care of the ghost in the park. Whitcombe-Sears had even helped. The banter between Corbin and Whitcombe-Sears had been so practiced that Jenny had been surprised when Corbin had sent her back to the library rather than go himself to see his old buddy.

Today was the first time she had visited since Corbin's death.

The vestibule hadn't changed much. The bulletin board still advertised various services and events happening around town, including one of the local schools putting on a production of *1776*. Jenny thought it would be hilarious to bring Crane to see that, just to watch his head explode.

She walked through the same security gate, walked past the same bookcases in place of pews, all stuffed to the gills with various and sundry musty tomes.

Approaching the main desk, she saw the biggest difference since the last time she was there: Whitcombe-Sears had finally upgraded. The computers were all brand-new and with flat-screen monitors instead of the monster cubes he'd had before.

The man himself had cut the ponytail off, which just emphasized how far his hairline had receded.

He looked up from reading his fancy new monitor and his eyes widened. "Goodness gracious, great balls of fire, if it isn't Jenny Mills! Didn't expect to see you again. I'd heard they, ah—"

"Put me away? Yeah, I was institutionalized for a while, but I'm *all* better now."

"You ask me, you were always crazy." He grinned, then dropped it quickly. "I guess that's why you weren't at the funeral?"

Jenny lowered her eyes. "Yeah. They don't give furloughs, not unless it's a family member."

Whitcombe-Sears shook his head. "Stupid rules. You and Corbin *were* family, in all the ways that mattered. Anyhow, that's neither here nor there. What can I do you for?"

"I actually want to take a look at your exhibits."

Frowning, Whitcombe-Sears said, "Since when do you care about art?"

"Oh, I really don't. But I read online that you have an Independence Cross on display."

"I have one on display, yes. Wanna see?"

"Please."

That got Whitcombe-Sears to blink in surprise.

"'Please'? Damn, being in the funny farm made you all polite and stuff."

Jenny actually credited Crane with any semblance of decorum she had. It was hard *not* to be polite around him. It was like he exuded a force field made out of manners.

But the last thing she wanted to do was try to explain Crane to—well, to anybody, really, so she just prompted Whitcombe-Sears. "Exhibit?"

"Right." He tapped something on his computer and then got up and led her to the area to the south wall on the left.

"I thought the restrooms were this way."

"They also are, yeah." Whitcombe-Sears grinned. "I've got a ton of family heirlooms, and I rotate 'em through the display cases."

He led Jenny through the doorway. She'd been through it before, but always to turn right and go down the stairs to the bathroom. This time she continued ahead a bit and turned left to find a small room filled with glass cases.

Ignoring everything else in the room—though a nice portrait caught her eye—she made a beeline for a piece of metal in the shape of a cross. The cross itself was even on all sides, and rather short, so it was more like the Red Cross logo than, say, a Catholic crucifix. It had a small loop on top of it, which was probably what a string or chain was run through so it could be worn around one's neck.

"The crosses were all forged by a French silversmith named Gaston Mercier," Whitcombe-Sears started in what Jenny had come to recognize as his lecture tone. "This one belonged to one of my ancestors, Caleb Whitcombe. He worked with Henry Knox to move cannons from Fort Ticonderoga to Boston, and set them up at Dorchester Heights. That helped win the Siege of Boston, which was one of the—"

"The first battles of the Revolutionary War, yeah, I know."

Whitcombe-Sears stared at Jenny dubiously. "Since when do you know about history, Jenny?"

"Let's just say I've developed a more than passing interest in the American Revolution." She squinted more closely at the cross, noticing what appeared to be scratches on the side, but after gazing more intently upon them, she realized there was a pattern to them. "What're those scratches?"

"Good catch. Anybody else came in here and asked that, they'd get the spiel about shipping and time passing and other nonsense. But lucky you, Jenny Mills, you get the *real* story. See, Gaston Mercier wasn't just a silversmith—he was an alchemist. He couldn't actually turn straw into gold, like other alchemists tried, but he learned how to infuse magic into solid objects. Especially silver, which conducts spellcraft quite efficiently. And there was a reason why Washington specifically chose Mercier for this commission."

Jenny steeled herself for another lecture.

SEVEN

Mount Vernon, Virginia

AUGUST 1785

GEORGE WASHINGTON PACED back and forth in the sitting room, waiting for the physician to finish his examination of his wife.

"Your perambulations are dizzying me, cousin," said Lund Washington, who managed the plantation for Washington, and had been one of his greatest confidants in the two years since the British conceded, recognized the independence of the thirteen states, and signed the Treaty of Paris. It had been a near thing, and Washington knew that victory was achieved as much due to King George III's concerns about turbulence in France—much closer to home—as it was Washington's own strategies.

Since resigning as commander in chief of the Continental Army after the treaty was signed, Washington had enjoyed the quiet life of a retired general, advising the thirteen states as they worked to determine what type of nation they would be.

"It should have been over, Lund."

"It is over, George. We were victorious. Or, at the very least, the Crown conceded."

"It is not the Crown that concerns me," Washington snapped. "It is the forces that allied themselves with the Crown against us." He turned to look out the large picture window that showed him his plantation, the crops struggling through an awful drought. "They do not take defeat well."

"There's been no sign of any retribution from the daemonic forces, have there?" Lund asked. He had been kept informed of the second front on which Washington had been fighting the war, as much due to fear of the very reprisals that he believed were now being visited upon his family.

"Earlier this year, Martha's brother Bartholomew died of a fever. Last month, her mother also died of a fever. Now Martha is ill with a fever, and I fear the worst."

Lund shook his head. "People get fevers, George. It's not—"

The physician chose that moment to exit from the bedroom, sparing Washington from whatever platitude Lund was about to utter, and Washington turned to face the short, stout, red-haired doctor.

"What news?"

Shaking his head, the doctor replied, "I cannot say, General. She burns with a fever the like of which

I've never seen. In truth, I've no idea how she clings to life with her bodily fires burning so brightly. The slaves are applying cloths wetted with cold at my direction, but I do not know what else may be done for her. I'll return in two days—please have your slaves continue to keep her cool. I recommend leaving the windows open wide at night as well."

"Thank you, Doctor."

After another of the slaves saw the physician out, Washington turned to his cousin. "Unnatural heat—the crops have also suffered thus."

Lund smiled. "I know that expression, cousin. You have a thought."

Washington let out a breath through his dentures. "Don't be boorish, Lund. The crops have suffered this summer due to excess heat. Bartholomew and Mother Dandridge both died of a fever, and now Martha suffers one. You'll notice, I'm sure, the common denominator in these events."

"Besides you? Heat."

"Yes. And there is one foe of ours, whom I thought was dispatched. A priestess named Serilda, who was granted the power of a daemon in Trenton in 1776 and took up residence in New York shortly thereafter, wreaking havoc on our cause. She destroyed settlements in Saratoga, Albany, Kingston, Peekskill, and Sleepy Hollow before she was burned at the stake. But she led a coven, and I believe that they are attempting to enact revenge."

Even as Washington spoke the words, the sun

seemed to disappear all of a sudden, as the room grew very dark. Washington ran to the window to see that the sun had been reduced to that of a ring around a small black circle.

A female voice sounded from everywhere in the house, yet Washington could see nobody except for himself and Lund. True, it was darker, but he could still see the sitting room, albeit faded, and even some of his crops through the window.

The voice sounded cold as death, and was definitely female despite how deep and resonant it was as it echoed.

Your precious wife will not live out the week, enemy of ours! Soon everything you hold dear will be gone, gone, gone!

"Show yourself, cowardly woman!"

Tomorrow, when the moon is new, I will take your love from you, and you will know suffering as you have never known before!

Then the sun started to brighten once again, and the voice disappeared.

Washington moved quickly after that, assigning his male slaves to guard the plantation, even going so far as to arm some of them. He had no idea if Serilda's minions would be affected by gunshot or bayonets, but they tended to employ human vessels, and those were vulnerable enough.

The following afternoon, however, a horseman arrived with a package. Lund met the messenger at the door prepared to turn him away—Washington had left strict instructions that he was not to be disturbed—but then the retired general recalled the letter he had received the previous week from France.

"Let him in!" Washington bellowed from Martha's bedside, and then he left her in the hands of the female slaves who continued to apply wetted cloth in a vain attempt to arrest the fever.

The rider smelled very much of horse, a stench that Washington found at once invigorating and nauseating. It reminded him far too much of the war. He wanted nothing more than to put the war behind him, to move forward with aiding in the creation of a republic.

The war, however, was apparently not quite ready to be put to rest.

"General Washington."

"Simply 'Mr. Washington' will suffice," Washington said quickly. He hadn't bothered to correct the doctor, but this messenger traveled all across the new nation, and might bring reminders of Washington's preference not to be referred to by a title he'd quit from two years previous.

"Very well then, Mr. Washington. The gentleman from France has finished his commission. He apologizes for the late—"

Reaching for the parcel the messenger held, Washington said, "Yes, yes, I read M'sieu Mercier's missive that he sent ahead of the commission."

"Of course, sir." The messenger allowed Washington to take the package from him. "I should also add that the gentleman emplaced the runes as you requested. He didn't feel it prudent to mention *that* in his letter."

"Understandable," Washington said gravely. He unwrapped the parcel, which had sailed across the Atlantic from Paris, arriving in the Port of Baltimore several days ago, and ridden here to Mount Vernon by the messenger.

Inside were the ten crosses that had been awarded a decade ago. For a moment, Washington thought of those who had not survived the interim since the Congressional Crosses were awarded. In particular, he thought sadly about Crane and van Brunt, and how their fates were intertwined. . . .

But now he had more pressing concerns. Each cross was individually wrapped in sackcloth and twine, and Washington started to untie the twine on one of them. "Lund, fetch the chalk and bring it to Martha's room."

The messenger cleared his throat. "If that will be all?"

He looked up in surprise at the messenger, having briefly forgotten the man's existence. "Sir, my apologies. Do you require refreshment, or—"

Holding up both hands, the messenger said, "That will not be necessary, sir, but thank you. I shall leave you to your work. I have already secured lodgings in Alexandria, and I shall proceed there once my mount has rested."

Placing the cross back in the box, Washington reached out to shake the messenger's hand. "Thank you, sir, for the great service you have done to these United States."

"The honor is mine, Gen—" He smiled. "Mr. Washington. My service is as nothing compared to yours."

After the messenger took his leave to sit with his horse until it was watered and rested enough to make the eight-mile journey to Alexandria, Washington brought the box into Martha's room. Lund joined him a moment later.

"How is she?" Washington asked the slave tending to her.

She shook her head. "She's doin' mighty poorly, sir. Fever's *still* ragin'."

"With luck, we can cure her soon."

Washington took the chalk from Lund, knelt down, and began drawing the sigil on the wooden floor in front of Martha's bed, hoping that he remembered it exactly as the Reverend Mr. Knapp had shown him. Ideally, he would have the reverend himself perform the ritual, as he was far better versed in such sorceries than Washington ever would be. Knapp had always said that Washington was far too much of a rationalist to give himself over to the power of the magic, and perhaps that was still true to some degree, despite everything he'd seen. If anything, seeing how the supernatural forces of the world fed on ignorance and passivity served to increase Washington's belief in self-determination. A republic where rule was by the people rather than tyrants was the only way to fight those forces. There was a reason why the daemons allied with monarchs and kings, after all.

But the reverend was in Sleepy Hollow, and it would take many days for him to arrive. Too many days. Martha didn't have that kind of time.

Washington had lost too many people who mattered to him over the years. He would not lose Martha as well.

After drawing the sigil, which resembled a star with six points, Washington looked up at his cousin as he got to his feet. "Help me unwrap the crosses, Lund. We only need six of them."

"Then why did you commission ten?"

"Because ten men earned them," Washington said sharply. Then he softened. "Besides, it is always prudent to have more than one needs."

Lund started unwrapping one of the medals. "Why six?"

"The Reverend Mr. Knapp explained to me that six is a powerful number when it comes to magics associated with life and death, as these runes are. There are six stages in life, after all: birth, infancy, childhood, adulthood, old age, and death."

Nodding, Lund unwrapped the remaining crosses with Washington in silence.

"Place each cross on one of the points of the symbol, Lund."

Lund nodded again and did as he was told.

By the time they were done, it was almost sunset. "Night will fall, and with it will rise a new moon."

"Does the new moon even rise?" Lund asked.

"Don't be doltish, Lund, of course it does, we simply cannot see it. And the minions of Serilda will make their final attempt on Martha when the moon rises, and we must be ready with the counter-spell."

The wait for the moon to rise was interminable. Washington remembered many campaigns where he and his troops had to wait for day to break or for night to fall or for supplies to arrive. War was sometimes an organized bore, with the added distraction of time seeming to slow down when there was nothing to do, particularly if one was waiting for something.

But at last the moon rose and night fell, and Washington began chanting the words from the *grimoire* that Knapp had lent him, and which he had retrieved from the library shortly after they prepared the floor.

Martha moaned with her fever, crying out mournfully, breaking Washington's heart with each utterance.

Then the deathly voice sounded again, even as a hot, fetid wind blew through the open windows of the bedroom. *You cannot stop me with your small spells!*

Washington continued to chant the words from the *grimoire*.

Your wife will die and you will suffer and you will never know happiness again! You will pay for what you did to Serilda!

Finally, Washington finished the incantation. Each of the Congressional Crosses he and Lund had placed on the sigil started to glow eerily. "The spell I have cast is not intended to stop you, witch. It is intended to save my wife."

For a moment, nothing happened. The wind continued, but the awful voice of Serilda's minion remained quiet.

Then the voice screamed loud enough to rattle Washington's very bones. *What have you* done*? I cannot touch her!*

The slave woman who'd been caring for Martha— and who'd been crossing herself repeatedly since nightfall—said, "Sir, the fever's goin' down!"

Curse you, George Washington! She had the touch of death upon her, and you removed it!

"That was the notion, yes. Begone, witch! There is nothing for you here."

I will go, the voice said, louder this time, and the wind picked up, feeling like a hot slap across Washington's face. *But know this, Serilda* will *rise again!*

With that, the wind died down, leaving only the usual humid Virginia air that Washington expected in early August.

Although the cold, dark voice was gone, he did hear a much weaker one speak from the bed.

"G-George?"

"Martha!" A wave of relief spread over Washington as he ran to his wife's side. She hadn't spoken a single word in almost a week.

"I—I feel *awful.*"

Washington actually allowed himself to finally laugh. He sat on the side of the bed and embraced Martha, holding her head to his breast. "Do not fret, Martha. You're safe now."

The next morning, Washington arranged to have the Congressional Crosses delivered to the recipients—or, failing that, to their relations. The only one who left no family behind—at least, none to whom such an award could be given—was Crane.

Washington would have to find a place to store that one until such a time as Crane himself would be able to collect it. . . .

EIGHT

New York City

JANUARY 2014

BEDRAJ DEZAN HATED traveling exhibits.

His job as head of security for the Museum of the City of New York meant that he had to make sure that all the exhibits were, well, secure. This included supervising the staff of guards who kept an eye on both patrons and exhibits, making sure the alarm systems were state-of-the-art and up-to-date—or, at least, as much as the budget allowed for—and generally keeping the building safe and secure.

And Bedraj was very good at his job. He was proud of their record since his hiring: no thefts, minimal vandalism, and the lowest number of patron-related incidents since the museum opened at its current Fifth Avenue location in 1932. The vaults were secure, and the transfers of pieces from the vaults to the exhibit halls were always flawless. He'd been on the job for almost twenty years, surviving the post-9/11 fanaticism about security—which actually enabled him to incorporate some upgrades that had been deemed excessive in 2000—as well as the changes that came with emerging technology.

He had everything down to a science, a well-oiled machine.

Except when traveling exhibits showed up.

They always had their own security arrangements, and they inevitably clashed with his own. They had alarms that they insisted on using that were incompatible with MCNY's own system. They'd insist on security measures that would require him to hire more people, except that the museum didn't have the budget to hire more people or pay overtime for existing employees to do it.

He also had a good relationship with the local Interpol office, the FBI's white-collar division, and the cops of the 23rd Precinct of the NYPD. Which made today's invasion of his museum by representatives from the latter somewhat annoying.

It started when he was going over some files in the security office on the fifth floor of the museum, and he got a radio call from Ahondjon, the guard who was working the desk at the main entrance to the museum.

"Bedraj, there's a bunch of folks from the NYPD here, along with Ms. Nugent from IYS. They'd like to talk to you."

Frowning, Bedraj told Ahondjon he'd be right down and took the elevator to the second floor and then took the grand Nathalie Pierrepont Comfort staircase down the rest of the way to the first floor so he had time to see what he was in for.

As he went down the large spiral staircase, he saw a trio of uniformed officers, and three more in plainclothes. He recognized two of the latter. The tall, lanky Latino man wearing a suit that didn't quite seem to fit right was Detective Tomas Vasquez from the 23rd Precinct. The short, stout woman with the olive skin and wearing a dark green suit that fit her perfectly despite her fireplug shape was the aforementioned Beth Nugent from the insurance company.

Once he hit the first-floor landing, he stared right at the detective. "Yeah, Tomas, what's going on?"

Tomas held up both hands. "We've got a credible threat, Bedraj. Can we go talk in your office?"

The three officers started wandering around the museum, one heading to the exhibit at the east end of the building, another to the southern hall, the third into the gift shop. They made both the customers and the other museum employees nervous.

After giving the uniforms a sidelong glance, Bedraj looked back at Tomas. "Yeah, okay. This way." He led the three of them to the elevator, and then he used his key to access the fifth floor. The top two floors of the museum were not open to the public.

They entered his cramped office, which had only two guest chairs. The tall guy offered to remain standing.

"That's very nice of you . . . ?"

"Sorry," Tomas said as he sat down, getting the hint. "Bedraj Dezan, head of security, meet Captain Frank Irving, from Sleepy Hollow. You already know Beth."

Bedraj sat in his chair, which made the same awful squeaking noise it always made. Beth, Tomas, and the captain from Westchester all winced at the noise, but the truth was, Bedraj didn't even notice it anymore. "Yeah, she's the reason I'm taking this meeting in my office instead of making you and your goons all pay admission."

Tomas winced. "Hey, c'mon, that's not fair. You know me, Bedraj, you know I wouldn't be doing this if I didn't think it was a good idea." Then he grinned. "Besides, it's suggested admission. You do that, I'll tell 'em to each pay a penny."

"Right." Bedraj shook his head. "Yeah, and Beth knows I know you, which is why it's you here instead of someone else from the two-three. So cut the crap and tell me what's going on."

For the first time, Irving spoke up. "Mr. Dezan, your current exhibit from the Society of the Cincinnati has an Independence Cross that was awarded to Tench Tilghman as part of the exhibit, am I right?"

"Of course it's right."

"The Metropolitan Museum of Art has two Independence Crosses, and the Cortlandt Museum in Tarrytown has another. All three have been stolen in the last week."

For the first time, Bedraj sat up in his chair and viewed this meeting as something other than an annoyance. He'd been humoring Tomas and Beth because of his past relationship with them, but now—now, this really *was* a credible threat.

"Yeah, normally, this'd be the part where I tell you we have state-of-the-art security—and on top of that, the Society put a webcam on the damn exhibit, so the whole world can see it 24/7—but the Met has even better security than we do." He gave Beth a glance.

She'd been uncharacteristically quiet up until now. "Look, Bedraj, SOP would be to go to the Society and MCNY's board for this, but I know you. I know you hate the crap they pull, and besides, this is a security matter. So we're doing you the courtesy of coming to you first."

Bedraj nodded. "I appreciate that, Beth."

Beth returned the nod. "Look, I know you don't have the money to hire more guards, so the two-three's gonna have three officers here during closing hours on foot patrol, and Frank and I'll be here, too."

A response died on Bedraj's lips at that last phrase. "Hang on. Beth, you I can make a case for, but—well, no offense, Captain, but you're way out of your jurisdiction."

"Only recently," he said. "I was NYPD before I transferred up to Sleepy Hollow. In fact," and for the first time, the captain's expression changed from the stony one he'd been using, "I used to be her partner. Taught her everything she knows."

Snorting, Bedraj said, "So it's *your* fault." He shook his head. "Yeah, I don't think I can allow it. I mean—"

"Mr. Dezan, they've already killed to achieve their goal."

"What!?" Nobody had told Bedraj anything about murder.

"Show him," Irving said to Beth, who pulled a tablet out of her purse.

Tomas shook his head. "No wonder you left the force, Nugent. We ain't got the budget for the nice toys."

Beth swiped her index finger across the tablet screen a few times and then showed Bedraj a gruesome photo of a bunch of body parts spread out across a lobby area.

As Bedraj's breakfast started to well up to his throat, Beth took the tablet back and swiped over to another photo, but he held a hand up. "Yeah, I get the idea."

"The vics," Irving said, "were the three security guards on duty at the Cortlandt. The other two looked like that guy."

"Dammit." Bedraj swallowed down bile. "Yeah, why exactly didn't you lead with that?"

"This kinda stuff," Beth said, indicating the tablet, "it's better to work your way up to."

"Says you." Bedraj shuddered. "Yeah, fine, come on over. We close at six, and thanks to the Sphincter of the Cincinnati"—the others chuckled at the malapropism—"I've got foot patrols overnight, but it's only two guards. If something that can do *that* wants the cross, I'm more than happy to make it seven."

"Good." Irving moved toward the door. "I've got some other business to take care of. I'll be back at six."

Tomas got up as well. "I've gotta get back to the house. I'm gonna leave my guys here until closing. Then I got three guys from the night shift coming in later, okay?"

Bedraj nodded, barely noticing Tomas and Beth follow Irving out the door.

All he could see was that dead security guard chopped to pieces.

He debated whether or not to tell the two overnight guards when they reported what they were in for. Jessica, he wasn't worried about, as she'd been a cop in Pittsburgh before she moved to New York for her husband's job. But Emmett was a retired stevedore who mostly just liked the quiet of the overnight. He didn't really sign on for being cut to pieces.

None of them did.

That was the great thing about museum security

work. It was mostly just dealing with stupid tourists who didn't get the concept of not touching things. The only criminals were either thieves or vandals.

But murderers? That was a whole other level.

Bedraj spent the rest of the day wandering around the museum trying not to be conspicuous. He didn't think he entirely succeeded, but it mostly didn't matter, because the three cops Tomas had left behind weren't even trying. The day's patrons were confused and nervous at the presence of NYPD in the building. For the first few years after the twin towers fell, it wasn't unusual to see a heavy police presence in any public building in town. If nothing else, it made people feel safer. But that had tapered off over the years, to the point where now such a presence made people *more* nervous.

He also made contact with the Society of the Cincinnati and the board to discuss the threat. Beth had been right in that it made his life easier this way. It looked like Bedraj did his job well, identifying the threat and bringing it to them instead of the other way around. They were grateful that Bedraj was already planning tighter security, and they all agreed to discontinue the webcam until the threat was passed. IT put up a message saying that there were technical problems with the feed, which Bedraj hoped wouldn't raise suspicions. The main thing was to cut off an avenue of surveillance for the thieves.

Bedraj was pretty much a wreck by the time six

o'clock rolled around. For almost two decades, he'd been keeping this place safe, but the worst thing that happened to anyone was that time a sculpture fell on a mover and broke the man's leg in four places (the sculpture survived unscathed). There was the occasional trip-and-fall, the occasional drunk or high students, but nobody had ever even gotten seriously hurt on his watch, much less killed.

At about five, he got a text from his wife, saying that she was home from her shift at the hospital and dinner was going to be lamb stew.

He loved Milena's lamb stew.

The three cops left and were replaced by three others, while both Jessica and Emmett reported for their shift.

At about a quarter past, Irving and Beth both showed up. They all stood at the foot of the Comfort staircase on the first floor, the front doors having been locked, the general public and staff all ushered out.

"We got this, Bedraj," Beth said with a small smile. "Get on home to Milena and the kids."

"Yeah, I can't." He shook his head, the phantom taste of the lamb stew on his lips. "First of all, it's just Milena—both boys are away at college now. And besides . . ." He sighed heavily. "I need to make a phone call. Excuse me." Pulling his smartphone from his pocket, he called their Bronx apartment.

As always, she answered in Armenian. "Yes, my love?"

In the same language, he replied, "My apologies, little flower, but I'm afraid I must remain late at work. There is a small crisis."

"What kind of crisis? Is everyone okay?"

Bedraj smiled. Milena was always thinking of other people first. "Everyone's fine—but I need to remain this evening and do another shift in order to make sure that everyone *remains* fine."

"Of course, my love. Be well. I will save some stew for you to heat up when you get home."

"Thank you, little flower. I love you."

"I love you, too."

Now Beth was staring at him angrily with her hands on her hips. "Okay, my Armenian's kinda rusty, but I'm pretty sure you just told Milena that you're not coming home tonight." She smirked. "This is how wives get suspicious of their husbands having affairs, y'know."

Bedraj rolled his eyes. "You know perfectly well that Milena has no such suspicions. Besides, if I went home to her, all I'd do is constantly text you for updates and not sleep and not enjoy her lamb stew."

Beth's eyes widened. "She's making her lamb stew and you're *still* staying here? They are not paying you enough for this, Bedraj."

Knowing that he'd have to fight to get the overtime request approved, a fight he was fairly certain he was going to lose, Bedraj agreed with her.

Jessica and Emmett walked up to him, Emmett lagging a bit behind and surreptitiously trying to hike his pants up, pushed down as they were by his prodigious beer gut.

"What's the badge party for, Bedraj?" Jessica asked.

Before Bedraj could reply, the captain from Westchester stepped forward. "I'm Captain Frank Irving from Sleepy Hollow. We believe that one of your pieces is being targeted by a thief who doesn't like it when security guards get in the way. He's already killed three people. Our job tonight is to make sure they don't get Tench Tilghman's Independence Cross."

Jessica got a dubious look on her face. "All the valuables up in here, and *that's* what they're after? What the hell for?"

"Your guess is as good as mine," Irving said, "but three others just like it have been stolen, with other merchandise left alone, and that's a good enough reason for us to not let him have this one. We're augmenting you two with three officers from the two-three, Ms. Nugent from IYS, myself, and Mr. Dezan."

"Great, a stakeout. Just like the good old days." Jessica was grinning.

Emmett wasn't. "Y'know, Bedraj, I ain't feelin' so good. I only didn't call in sick 'cause I didn't wanna leave Jess alone, but looks like you're covered, so if it's all'a same to you . . ."

Now Jessica was rolling her eyes. "For cryin' out loud, Emmett, grow a pair, willya please?"

Putting his hands on his large hips, Emmett said, "I got me a pair, Jess. And I wanna *keep* 'em. 'Sides, even Bedraj is stayin'."

"Gave up Milena's lamb stew, too," Beth said with a twinkle in her eye.

That, in turn, made Emmett's eyes go wide. "Oh, *hell*, no. If you're *that* worried, I don't want no part'a this. Overnight gig's supposed to be cushy. I retired from the docks so I wouldn't have to risk my life no more."

Jessica was about to object again, but Bedraj interrupted. "It's fine, Emmett, go home. It'll come out of your sick leave."

A look of relief washed over Emmett's face, his shoulders slumping. "*Thank* you, Bedraj. I owe you one. Hell, I owe you *six*." He turned and practically ran out the door.

Beth chuckled. "And then there were seven."

"It's fine," Jessica said. "Only thing he was good for was being a second set of eyes when I take a piss. So what's the plan?"

Bedraj had actually been thinking about it all day, and the plan he came up with would work just fine—he just put himself where he'd originally put Emmett. "Captain, Beth, I think you two should stay on the third floor—that's where the cross is, in the south gallery."

Irving nodded. "Makes sense."

"Sure, that's perfect," Beth added.

"I'll stay up on five and monitor everyone and

keep an eye on the roof, since that's an access point. Jessica, you and the three officers do roving patrols of the other floors."

"That's four people for six floors," Jessica said.

"No," Bedraj said slowly, "that's four people for four floors. Captain Irving and Beth will be on three and I'll be on five. The rest of you will cover the ground floor, the first floor, the second floor, and the fourth."

"Why bother with the ground floor?" Beth asked. "It's just got the kids' thing, right?"

Bedraj nodded. Beth was referring to the Frederick A. O. Schwarz Children's Center. "Yeah, c'mon, Beth, you know as well as I that thieves tend to come in from either above or below. I think the ground floor or the fifth is our most likely point of entry."

She shrugged. "Fair enough."

"Everyone stay in touch via radios." He had gathered up spare radios for the cops and Beth. "I know you all have your own radios, but these are all on the right frequency. Just easier."

Irving nodded and took his. "Thank you, Mr. Dezan. Good work."

"Yeah, thank *you*, Captain. I'm glad you alerted us to this threat so we could be prepared. Let's get to work."

The elevators were shut down for the night—another security measure—so Bedraj took the stairs up. The staircase was decorated with sayings about the city, good and bad, from a variety of sources. His favorite was always the one between the second and third floor from John Adams in 1774: "New Yorkers talk very loud, very fast, and all together. If they ask you a question, before you can utter three words of your answer, they will break out upon you again, and talk away."

For the first six hours after he settled down at the fifth-floor security station, all was quiet. Each of the seven of them got a dinner break—they got food from Chalsty's Café on the second floor—with only one person eating at a time. Any time some-one needed the bathroom, they did an entire run of their assigned area first before using the facilities.

And then the clock on the monitor of his com-puter went to midnight and all the lights in the en-tire museum went out.

Frowning, Bedraj reached for his cell phone, only to discover that he could still see by the light of his illuminated keyboard. The computer had been showing him the feeds from the security cameras when the screen went dark, but when he Alt-Tabbed over to Adobe Acrobat, it showed him the report he was reading earlier.

But his desk lamp no longer was working. He tried flicking it on and off several times, but it was no longer emitting light.

He grabbed his radio. "Everyone report in. Ir-ving."

The Westchester cop said, "Whole room's gone dark."

"Nugent."

"Same out here in the hallway," the insurance investigator said. "Flashlight ain't working, either."

Everyone else reported the same thing.

Jessica added, "Just looked out a window. All the buildings to the north on Fifth are lit up, so it ain't a power outage."

"What about to the south?" That was Beth.

Bedraj shook his head, even though no one could see it. "To the south is Mount Sinai Hospital. They've got their own generator so their having lights doesn't mean as much. All right, everyone stay where you are and move slowly toward—"

"AAAAAAAAAAAAAHHHHHHHHH-HHH!"

To Bedraj's horror, he had no idea whose scream that was. He'd never heard anyone scream quite like that before.

One of the cops cried out, "Xander! Xander, what happened? Wha—AAAAAAAAAAAAH-HHHHHHHHHHHHH!"

The two cops in question were on the ground floor and the first floor. Jessica was on the second. "Jessica, keep an eye out, the—"

He was interrupted by the sound of several shots being fired. Then: "AAAAAAAAAAAAAAH-HHHHHHHHHHH!"

Bedraj recognized the third scream instantly, even though he'd never actually heard Jessica scream.

Alt-Tabbing over to the control center for the museum, he turned the elevators back on. No way was he going to try to take the stairs in the dark, and if the electricity was working, he'd be able to get down faster in the elevator, especially since one of them was already up on five with him.

Getting up from his loud, squeaky chair, Bedraj ran toward the door and promptly slammed his knee into the side of his desk. "Sonofabitch!" He limped his way more slowly to the door, knives of pain slicing through his left knee as he hobbled forward.

Feeling his way across the hallway wall until he reached the elevator, he pressed the down button and the door opened right away, even making the dinging sound. Using his phone screen as a flashlight—the actual flashlight app wouldn't work, but the screen still lit up—he found the third-floor button and waited very not-patiently for it to ding down two flights.

When the doors opened, he was surprised that he could see in the hallway. Irving and the third cop were standing with their weapons out, the former in front of one of the two sets of glass doors on the far end of the hallway, which led to the Society of the Cincinnati's exhibit.

Then he saw Beth Nugent lying on the floor. "What happened?"

"I heard Beth cry out, and I found her like this," Irving said. "But nobody has moved past me."

The cop said, "I heard the same thing."

Bedraj nodded. "Officer, check on her. Captain, you need to stay with the cross. I'll go downstairs and"—he swallowed—"see what happened to the others."

He started to move toward the staircase, figuring that if the hallway was illuminated again, maybe the stairs would be as well.

Then he heard a scream from the end of the hall-way.

No, not a scream, a curse.

Turning, he saw Irving running out of the glass door. The security guard in him wanted to berate Irving for using the near door, which was supposed to be the entrance—the far door was the exit. It was their way of dealing with crowd control, and he had no idea why his brain decided to go there *now* of all places.

"The cross is *gone!*" The captain looked furious. "There's *no* way anyone could've gotten past me."

Shaking his head, Bedraj muttered, "This is a damn nightmare." He couldn't do anything about the cross yet, as he had to find out what happened to Jessica and the other two cops.

The staircase was still lit, and he ran down two

flights to the first floor, running out into the hall-way to see an arm on the floor.

It wasn't until he looked in the gift shop that he saw Jessica's head, her dead eyes staring right at him, her mouth open with the scream he'd heard over the radio.

Bedraj turned and ran toward the restrooms as the dinner he'd eaten at the café came welling up his throat. Bizarrely, his first thought was that he was glad he didn't eat Milena's lamb stew, as it would have been a shame to throw it up.

He also wished he'd gone home. A nervous wreck he might have been, but if he'd been spared the sight of one of his employees looking like *that*, and then throwing up all over the marble floor of the museum . . .

NINE

TICONDEROGA, NEW YORK

JANUARY 2014

ABBIE SPENT MOST of the drive up Interstate 87 to Ticonderoga being simultaneously charmed by Crane and seriously wanting to strangle him.

Thinking about it, that defined a lot of her relationship with him.

While they drove through Albany, Crane was going on about his previous visit to Ticonderoga.

"The Crown had actually renamed the fort after the region, but we had continued to refer to it by its French name of Fort Carillon, particularly once the fort was taken. There were only a few score men stationed there when Ethan Allen and Benedict Arnold stormed the place one early spring morning."

As much to reassure Crane that she was paying attention to his babbling as anything, Abbie said, "I'm assuming that's *before* Arnold turned traitor?"

Archly, Crane replied, "Strictly speaking, Lieutenant, *I* 'turned traitor.' Benedict had his reasons for what he did, just as I had mine."

"I'm sure he did. But most of the history that's been written since your time portrays him as one of the big villains of the revolution."

"As you and I both know, the truly 'big villains' were not recorded in your history books at all. In any event, I was not present for that particular battle, though I reported there the following winter alongside Henry Knox. Our task was to remove several cannon from the fort to Boston. Caleb Whitcombe was with us as well, and he expressed grave concern over leaving Fort Carillon poorly defended. Knox did insist that the defense of Boston was of more import." Crane smiled ruefully. "As it happens, both Whitcombe and Knox were correct. The fort *was* inadequately defended—it was taken without a shot by General Burgoyne—but the cannon *were* required at Boston."

"How many did you take with you?"

"Approximately sixty tons of cannon, and other artillery."

Abbie turned her eyes briefly from the road to shoot Crane a surprised glance. "Seriously? Without railroads? Or, hell, *roads*?"

Crane's smile was proud now. "Mr. Knox was quite the logistical genius. It was an amazing operation, one that many assumed would fail horribly, but Knox prepared for every eventuality. Indeed, one of Whitcombe's complaints was that we were trying to move the items in winter, when we'd be bogged down by snow. But we would have been far more greatly bogged by the rivers and swamps on the route that were conveniently frozen over."

This prompted a lengthy recitation of the pitfalls and problems they encountered over the three-month journey from Ticonderoga to Boston, which Abbie had to admit to only halfway paying attention to, as it was getting very late at night, she'd been driving for hours, and she needed all of her focus to stay awake and watch the road.

Eventually they arrived at Ticonderoga, and checked into a cheap motel with two double beds. The carpet had worn down enough that she could see most of the underflooring, the place was last painted during the Reagan administration, the so-called art on the wall was hideous even by hotel room standards, and when she sat on one of the beds, she could feel the springs through the sheets and her jeans.

But she could afford it, which was what mattered.

"We shall get a good night's rest, Lieutenant," Crane said enthusiastically, "and then on the morrow we shall visit this re-creation of Fort Carillon that you and the captain spoke so highly of. I must confess to anticipation."

"Really? I hadn't noticed." Abbie smirked.

"Your sarcasm is noted, and not appreciated,"

Crane said tartly. "I have observed that, while lacking in several specific details, many of the re-creations in the Hudson Valley are more or less satisfactory, given the passage of time. I eagerly await observation of what the Pell family have accomplished."

Abbie frowned. "Who?"

"According to what I was able to ascertain on the Internal Net—"

"Internet," Abbie corrected automatically.

"—the land on which the fort had existed was sold to the Pell family after the war. They were responsible for the reconstruction of the fort and the conversion of it to an attraction for alien visitors."

"A tourist trap." Abbie got up from the uncomfortable bed. "After that drive I need a shower. The fort isn't actually open this time of year, but we're meeting up with a local cop and one of the docents to take us around."

"Excellent."

Abbie tossed and turned the entire night. Crane, of course, slept quietly.

"How do you *do* that?" a bleary-eyed Abbie asked as they went to the lobby so Abbie could obtain a desperately needed caffeine infusion.

"Do what?"

"Sleep on that collection of metal springs really badly disguised as a mattress."

"I slept on much less comfortable surfaces during

my time at war, Lieutenant. By comparison, even that poorly disguised mattress is the lap of luxury."

"If you say so," she muttered, and then ordered the largest coffee the place would give her.

She checked in with Irving and Jenny while drinking her coffee and chowing down on a muffin. Her sister had nothing new beyond what Whitcombe-Sears had told her last night—including how George Washington used the six crosses for a spell that staved off death—but the captain did have news and it was all bad. The cross at MCNY had been stolen at midnight, with two NYPD cops and one MCNY security person killed in the same grisly manner as the three security guards in Tarrytown. Irving was fine, as was his ex-partner, MCNY's security chief, and the third cop who'd been assigned, but Tench Tilghman's medal was gone.

In light of this, Irving also assigned two uniforms to the Whitcombe-Sears Library and had a patrol car drive by regularly.

It was a short drive over to Fort Ticonderoga for Abbie and Crane. However, they'd barely started down Wicker when Crane, noticing something up ahead, asked, "May we pull to the side, please?"

Following Crane's glance, she saw a bronze statue in the midst of a traffic circle at the intersection of Wicker Street and Montcalm Street. "Hang on," Abbie said, and turned right onto Montcalm, pulling into a diner's driveway.

They exited the car and then walked back to the traffic circle. Now that she wasn't driving and searching for somewhere to park, Abbie took a more significant look at it. The statue itself was a woman with her left hand upraised. At the base of the statue were four figures.

"I read of this," Crane said as they approached it. "The figure atop is representative of liberty. The four figures at the base are a Scotsman, a French-man, an Iroquois, and a British colonist—or, rather, American, as you'd say now."

Abbie nodded. "Represents the region's history nicely, doesn't it?"

"Indeed." He turned to Abbie and smiled. "Thank you for the indulgence, Lieutenant. Shall we proceed?"

They got back into the car and continued down Montcalm. En route they passed a small star-shaped structure—the exact configuration of the fort, as it happened. Crane did a comical double take, but Abbie just smiled. "Irving told me about the sewage plant over there."

"Sewage plant?"

"Yup. They built it scaled down from the same specs as the fort."

"How droll. Based on what I read of the Pell family, not to mention the statue we just saw, I thought the people of this village to be more respectful of their history."

"The fort's not the only history," Abbie said. "In

the nineteenth and twentieth centuries, there was a big paper mill here. I used to think they made pencils, too, since every standardized test I took was with a pencil that said TICONDEROGA on the side." She shrugged. "Turns out those were made from a mine about twenty-five miles from here, and the wood came from somewhere else entirely."

When they arrived at the parking lot adjacent to the fort, Abbie pulled her car in next to the blue cruiser from the Ticonderoga Police Department and a battered, brown midsized SUV. Both had plenty of white residue on the underside from driving on roads that had been covered in salt to melt snow and ice.

As they approached the star-shaped fort itself, Crane started getting what Abbie had started to think of as his disapproving face, last seen when he heard a tour guide misrepresenting Paul Revere's midnight ride.

But before he could complain about whatever new slight he'd found, they were greeted by a tall young man wearing a police uniform, and a stooped-over old man with much paler skin than the cop, who wore a black wool coat and carried a wooden cane. It didn't take Abbie's skills as a detective to work out who had the cop car and who had the beat-up SUV.

Looking at the cop, Abbie said, "You must be Investigator Ruddle."

"Call me Paul." Ruddle reached out a hand,

which Abbie shook. She'd been amused to learn that the Ticonderoga Police Department used the title of "investigator" rather than "detective."

"I'm Lieutenant Abbie Mills, and this is our consultant, Professor Ichabod Crane."

After giving Abbie a firm handshake, Ruddle did the same with Crane. "A pleasure, Professor Crane. Where do you teach?"

"Oxford, though I'm on sabbatical at present in order to consult on Lieutenant Mills's ongoing investigation."

The older man gave a papery chuckle. "I like that—'left-tenant.' That's so British."

"This," Ruddle said, "is Theodore Provoncha. He's one of the docents of the fort."

"Call me Teddy. So I'm told that you people think someone's out to steal our Independence Cross."

"I'd say it's definite, Mr. Provoncha," Abbie said.

Provoncha smiled. "Please, it's Teddy."

Abbie did not return the smile. "The point is, four other Independence Crosses have been stolen, with six murders as collateral damage."

That got Provoncha's face to fall. "Oh my goodness. That's horrible."

"We agree," Abbie said. "That's why we'd like to augment your security."

"I don't know about that." Provoncha started walking toward the fort. "But let me show you around the place, and show you our security."

"That would be great."

As they approached the fort's interior—which Abbie really hoped was heated, as it was about ten degrees colder up here than it was in Sleepy Hollow—Crane said, "Excuse me, Mr. Provoncha—"

"Please, it's Teddy. You folks from downstate are too damn formal. I blame the city, myself."

"Be that as it may—Teddy, I wonder if you can explain to me how you are permitted to refer to this monstrosity as a re-creation of Fort Carillon."

"It's actually Fort Ticonderoga," Provoncha said. "Carillon was the French name. The British changed the name when they took it during the French and Indian War."

"Yes, and after the Seven Years' War—God knows how the other phrase came to be—the colonists continued to refer to it by the name given it by their allies, the French, rather than the name given it by the Crown, their enemies. Regardless, this looks *nothing* like the fort as it was during the revolution."

"Well, it does have the same configuration—"

"Oh, bravo, you managed to re-create the fort's largest distinguishing feature, but at the expense of verisimilitude *anywhere* else. It was not all stonework, for a start, the emplacements are *mis*placed, and—"

"Surprised you know so much about it," Provoncha interrupted as they went through a passage to the interior courtyard. "What is it you teach at Oxford?"

"History," Crane said tightly, "with an emphasis on the Revolutionary War period."

"Surprised you call it that." Provoncha smiled. "I always heard that you Brits referred to it as the colonial revolt or some such. Also surprised you teach it, since your side lost and all."

They arrived in the courtyard, which Abbie thought was beautiful, but just seemed to annoy Crane more.

"The only 'side' I'm on, sir, is that of the truth. This courtyard was never this wide open, as it was used for storage."

Provoncha stood right in the center of the open area, the early-morning sun casting long shadows from the fort's walls. "You have to understand, Professor, they didn't have cameras back in those days, so the Pell family, who did the reconstruction work back a hundred years ago, only had old drawings to go on. And—well, not to put too fine a point on it, but people weren't as all-fired concerned with hundred percent accuracy back in those days. As for this courtyard, we like to keep it as an open space, 'cause this is where we have a lot of our workshops, not to mention our fife-and-drum corps."

"Fife and drum?"

Bursting into a huge smile, Provoncha said, "Oh yes, they're quite impressive. During the season, they come out and perform several times a day, and they've traveled the world. They played at the 1939

World's Fair and the 1980 Winter Olympics. Just an amazing group, playing standards of the eighteenth and nineteenth centuries."

That brought Crane up short. Abbie couldn't help but smile. And also shiver, as they were still outside. She was starting to understand why the fort was open to the public only in the warm-weather months.

"What standards might those be?"

Provoncha chuckled. "Tell you what, when this is over, I'll give you a CD."

"I look forward to hearing it. Still—"

"Still," Abbie said quickly, "for now we've got bigger problems." She gave Crane a look.

To his credit, he looked contrite. "Of course, Lieutenant."

"Come on this way," Provoncha said, leading the four of them the rest of the way across the courtyard and then slowly up a flight of steps. With his cane, Provoncha took them slowly, so Abbie waited at the bottom of the stairs.

Crane dogged Provoncha's steps, asking what instruments the fife-and-drum corps played.

Ruddle shot Abbie a glance. "He always like that?"

"Not at all." She smiled. "Sometimes he's pedantic."

Laughing, Ruddle said, "Uh huh. Consultants are always a pain in the ass, ain't they?"

"Oh, he has his moments. I can honestly say I wouldn't have survived the past few months without him."

Once Provoncha and Crane got to the top of the stairs, Abbie and Ruddle followed suit. "Now then," Provoncha said, unlocking the door to one of the galleries, "this is where we keep the mementos of the removal of the cannon from this fort to Boston for the Siege of Boston."

Abbie winced. They had just gotten Crane *off* the subject. . . .

The room was decorated with fake wood on the walls that made the room look like it was trying to be a log cabin. There were display cases all over, painted with yellow trim, containing various items ranging from weapons to uniforms to jewelry to other decorative arts.

Crane found himself drawn to a weapons display, which included a flintlock musket and a flintlock pistol, both hanging in the open. Most of the exhibits were under glass, but the two weapons were simply hanging on hooks. Abbie hoped they were better secured when the museum was in season.

After staring at the pistol, and at the "Brown Bess" rifle, which had a bayonet attached to the top of the muzzle, Crane turned to Provoncha. "These are remarkably well preserved. Almost as if they haven't changed in two and a half centuries."

Abbie couldn't help but notice the wistful tone in Crane's voice when he uttered that last sentence.

"Well, to be honest, we're pretty sure those two were never fired. They were donated by a wealthy local who found them in her attic. She suspects that one of her ancestors purchased or was issued the weapons and never had the chance to use them in combat. It's hard to believe now, but these weapons marked the pinnacle of firearms technology in their day. They seem quaint and antiquated now, but being able to fire a musket ball from a distance changed the very face of combat."

"Yes," Crane said dryly, "I'm familiar with the intricacies of the weapons of the era."

Provoncha shook his head. "Sorry, occupational hazard. I walk into this room, I go into tour-guide mode. Anyhow, the Independence Cross you wanted to know about is right over here."

He led them to a display case. Abbie saw a portrait of Henry Knox, identifying him as the first-ever United States secretary of war. A placard described the removal of sixty pounds of cannon from Ticonderoga and bringing them to Boston, which Crane had mentioned in the car.

To Abbie's relief, Crane didn't carry on about any inaccuracies in the text. Instead, he stared at the cross. It was a simple piece of metal that looked just like the Red Cross logo, with each spoke of the cross of equal length. Abbie pointed and asked, "What are the scratches on the side?" It was a deliberately obtuse question, since she knew from Al Whitcombe-Sears via Jenny that they were runes.

"Not sure." Provoncha shrugged. "Prob'ly some kind of design the French silversmith preferred."

"Excuse me?"

Abbie whirled around, her hand instinctively going for her weapon. She saw a woman in her late thirties or early forties standing in the same doorway they'd come in.

However, Provoncha's face brightened, and Ruddle didn't seem put out by the woman's presence. Her status as friendly was confirmed by Provoncha's words. "Oh, hello, Stacy!"

"What're you doing here, Teddy? And Paul? What's going on?" Stacy seemed genuinely confused.

"Sorry, Stacy, but these people are from Sleepy Hollow, and they're looking into some thefts. Turns out the other medals like Henry Knox's Independence Cross were stolen, and they're worried that this one'll be targeted next."

"All the others are in New York, aren't they? Or in D.C.?"

Crane spoke up. "Actually, they are all in New York or its environs at present, as the one from the District of Columbia was in a traveling exhibit. And that was one of the ones that was taken."

"Yeah, but they're all down in New York." Stacy was oddly insistent.

Something felt off to Abbie. And then it hit her. "How'd you get here?"

Stacy blinked. "Excuse me?"

"There's only one parking lot, and it's got Teddy's car in it, as well as Paul's cruiser. Only way you could be surprised to see the two of them is if you came here some other way, or were already here before we all arrived. Unless you decided to take a stroll in twenty-degree weather."

Provoncha turned to face Abbie. "Lieutenant Mills, what're you getting at? Look, I get that you're a police officer and naturally suspicious, but I know Stacy, and she'd never—" He cut himself off and suddenly stumbled forward. Abbie noticed that he was suddenly sweating. While the gallery wasn't as cold as it was outside, it was still chilly enough that he shouldn't have been sweating.

Ruddle stepped forward. "Teddy, you okay?"

"I—"

Then Provoncha started to burn. Smoke wisped off his clothes, and then a fire started somewhere under his maroon sweater. Abbie watched in horror and disgust as it spread quickly, until suddenly his entire body was enveloped in flame. He only had time for a brief attempt at a scream before he burned to ash. The fire died as quickly as it expanded, leaving only a pile of black ash on the floor.

Stacy shook her head. "I never liked that old fart. Or anybody else in this *stupid* podunk town."

"Freeze." Abbie whipped her Glock out and pointed it right at Stacy. After a one-second hesitation, Ruddle did so with his service weapon, which appeared to be a Smith & Wesson. He wasn't holding it particularly steadily, but then he probably had much less experience with weird-ass deaths than Abbie had.

In fact, Abbie had had experience with this specific type of weird-ass death, not long after she first met Crane.

"Oh, please." Stacy rolled her eyes. "Do you really expect that to stop me?"

"Let's find out." Abbie squeezed the trigger.

Suddenly, Abbie felt a huge burst of heat that made her stumble backward. She recovered after a second, but a sizzling sound made her look down. Liquid metal was warping and burning the hardwood floor.

Stacy was unharmed.

"I can melt the bullets the same way I combusted old Teddy. Or, of course, I can just make the gunpowder go off in the gun."

Ruddle suddenly screamed and dropped his gun to the floor, shaking his hand up and down. "Damn, that got hot!"

Abbie heard the report of the weapon firing and then the pistol itself exploded. She threw her hands up to protect her face, and she felt something cut through her right arm. The pain wasn't too bad, but it made it hard for her to maintain her grip on the Glock.

Ruddle was now kneeling on the ground, his kneecap a bloody mess.

"See, when you heat up the gun itself," Stacy was saying in the same tone as your average tour guide, "and there's one in the chamber? It goes off. Isn't that right, Paul?"

"That's quite enough of that." That was Crane, who was now standing behind Stacy while holding the "Brown Bess" rifle.

Stacy turned to face Crane and laughed. "Seriously? First of all, even if that gun was loaded, I think we just established that it can't hurt me. Secondly, that gun *isn't* loaded, and hasn't been since around the War of 1812. So what, exactly, do you think you're gonna do with that thing?"

"This," Crane said as he lunged forward and stabbed Stacy right in the chest with the rifle's bayonet.

A very surprised Stacy collapsed to her knees. "Okay, didn't see that coming," she said in a weak voice.

Crane pulled the bayonet out, dropped the rifle, and moved to her side to guide her more gently to the floor on her back.

For her part, Abbie pulled out her cell phone and called 911.

Stacy laughed, but it was a gurgling, pathetic laugh, muffled as it was by all the blood in her mouth. "You really think you can stop us again, Witnesses?"

"You know who we are?" Crane asked.

"Course I do. Have ever since you stopped the mistress's resurrection on the last blood moon."

Abbie heard Stacy's comment just as she hung up with the 911 dispatcher, and then clutched her injured right arm with her left hand. It would be about ten minutes until the ambulance arrived. Stacy and whoever else was involved with this must have been part of the coven of Serilda of Abaddon, the witch Moloch tried to resurrect the previous October.

"Of course," Crane was saying, having obviously come to the same conclusion. "She killed Mr. Provoncha in the same manner that Serilda murdered poor Mr. Furth." He looked down at Stacy. "But the security guards at the museums were killed in a far different manner."

After coughing up some more blood, Stacy said, "We didn't all follow the mistress's path. And there are many kinds of magic to study."

"So why do you need the crosses?" Abbie asked.

"You'll find out soon enough." Stacy coughed up some more blood, then her body went limp in Crane's arms.

"She's gone." Crane gently let her down onto the floor and stood up, her blood on his hands.

Abbie shook her head ruefully. "We're gonna have a fun time explaining this one."

"Don't—don't worry," came a whispery voice from across the room.

Turning, Abbie saw that Ruddle was about to go

into shock, though he had had the presence of mind to use his coat to apply pressure to the wound on his kneecap. "Paul, it's okay, the bus is en route."

Ruddle nodded. "I know, I—I heard you call 'em. Look, Abbie, we've gotta—gotta have a cover story. Say—say Stacy went crazy, set stuff on fire, shot me. Also—you gotta gimme the rifle."

Frowning, Abbie asked, "Why?"

"So my—my prints'll be on it."

"Sir," Crane said, "I cannot allow you to—"

"Yes, you can," Ruddle said insistently. "No one'll question it if it's me."

Abbie shook her head. "Yeah, but Crane's prints will still be on it."

Ruddle nodded. "Right, he—he took it from me when—when I started—started goin' into shock. Look, everyone here knows—knows me. No one'll doubt my word, 'specially after—after being shot."

Abbie put a hand on Ruddle's shoulder. "Thanks, Paul, we owe you one."

"Yeah, well—alternative's to say a witch burned Teddy to death and your foreign buddy killed her. Don't think either'a those'd go—go over too good, y'know?" He managed a ragged smile, which Abbie returned.

She turned to Crane, who handed the "Brown Bess" over to Ruddle so he could get his fingerprints all over the stock. "We'll give our statement, and then get back home."

"After," Crane added quickly with a glance at her arm, "you get yourself tended to by the local physicians."

"Fine, *after* that we'll head back ASAP. If Serilda's coven's still active and stealing George Washington's magical medals, we gotta figure out why, and fast."

TEN

SLEEPY HOLLOW

JANUARY 2014

CRANE THOUGHT THE day had gotten as bad as it could when he saw one of Serilda of Abaddon's coven burn an innocent old man alive and cause a life-changing injury to a member of Ticonderoga's constabulary.

He did not reckon with the slow, painful process of bureaucracy. First he had to report to the emergency medical technicians who treated Investigator Ruddle's knee and Lieutenant Mills's arm. The latter, he was relieved to learn, was minor and treated with relative ease.

Then there was the report to Ruddle's fellow officers in the Ticonderoga Police Department, and then providing the same report to their supervisors, and again to a county prosecutor.

By nightfall, however, Crane and Mills were

permitted to leave, and also told that they might be called back up to testify in a court of law, though the prosecutor who told them that also said it was unlikely. "It looks to me like it was clean."

Once he and Mills got into the car, Crane said, "There are many adjectives I would use to describe what occurred this morning at the fort, Lieutenant. *Clean* would not be one of them."

"Yeah." Mills shook her head. "I also talked with the sergeant in charge, and he told me that they found all kinds of weird stuff in Stacy's apartment. They're thinking satanic cult."

"They would be halfway correct."

Mills started the vehicle's motor and proceeded on the roads through Ticonderoga that would take them back to the highway that would lead them back to Sleepy Hollow. "Gotta give you credit, Crane, you kept nicely to the cover story. Wasn't sure you'd be that good a liar."

Crane sat up straight in the passenger seat. "Why would you think that?"

"Really?" Mills smiled. "The man who took months to remember *not* to tell total strangers that he fought in the Revolutionary War?"

"I believe I may be excused a certain disorientation upon arrival in your century, Lieutenant. In any event, I was, you will recall, a soldier. The craft of war is one of many falsehoods. Spycraft was developed in order to make fighting a war more efficient, and I'm only a bit proud to say that I was an excellent spy. In fact, General Washington was one of the greatest mendicants in the colonial army."

"Which is funny, since one of the stories people tell about him is that he couldn't tell a lie."

"Even leaving aside the many falsehoods he had to perpetrate to keep the truth of the daemonic war he and I and others fought alongside the human one from the people, Washington's strategies were often based on deception. He was far from the greatest tactician the world has ever known, but he made up for it with guile. Often, he would convince the regulars that he was better equipped, better manned, better armed than he actually was. Deception is the heart of war, Lieutenant."

"I guess when you put it that way, sure." Mills sighed. "Unfortunately, we couldn't convince the people that run the fort to let us have the cross, but they are hiding it away and reporting it missing. We know Serilda's minions need one more, and they probably think we have the one that was in the fort. If we can keep the one in Sleepy Hollow away from them, we might be able to keep them from doing whatever the hell it is they're doing."

"We can but hope."

Crane manipulated the levers on the side of the car's passenger chair that enabled it to recline—a miraculous function that Crane was amazed to see everyone take for granted—and he fell asleep. Though unlike the lieutenant, he had slept through the previous night, he'd found the day's duties exhausting. Not so much being forced to inflict bodily harm on another. He regretted being forced into that action, but the witch herself had proven to have no regard for life, and the power to marry that lack of regard to fatal action. He doubted that he, the lieutenant, and the other constable would have survived the encounter had he not taken the drastic action.

No, what fatigued him was the bureaucratic nonsense, which had grown by leaps and bounds in the past two centuries.

He was awakened by the sound of the lieutenant's cell phone making a noise. At this point, they were only an hour or so from their destination. She took advantage of Crane's newly wakened state and her desire to see what telephonic communication she'd received to pull into one of the many restaurants that were operated by the McDonald family.

After she stopped the car, Mills stared at her phone. "Czierniewski. Great." As they went into the restaurant, Mills entered the code that would connect her to the barrister in question. "Hey, Phil. Yes, I *know* the trial's tomorrow. Yes, I'm out of town today, it's called police business. You'll be shocked to learn that I have other things on my plate besides a B-and-E from 2012. Don't worry, I'll be there at ten a.m. sharp." She ended the call as they approached the ordering table. "Bad enough I had to drive to Ticonderoga and back; tomorrow I get to put on my best suit and head to White Plains to testify in the Ippolito case."

"Ah, yes, part of the trial by jury. I might be interested in viewing this proceeding, to see how jurisprudence has evolved in the past two and a half centuries."

Mills grinned. "Well, for starters, nobody wears powdered wigs anymore."

"Thank heaven for that."

After their repast, they continued down the thoroughfare known as the New York State Thruway until they crossed the Tappan Zee Bridge.

"Someday, Lieutenant, you must inform me who precisely thought it wise to build a bridge across one of the widest expanses of the Hudson River. Might it not have been more sensible to construct it over one of the narrower passages?"

"Had nothing to do with how wide the river is, but where it is. They needed to build a bridge as close to New York City as possible, but it had to be north of the New Jersey border."

"Whyever for?"

"Politics. Any bridge between New York and New Jersey is controlled by the Port Authority, which is administered by both states. They tried, but they couldn't get the bridge done, so New York built the Tappan Zee here."

Crane was disgusted. "During the war, without interstate cooperation, we would never have won. Fort Carillon, to give an example from the location we just left—we would never have taken it were it not for the cooperation of a Massachusetts regiment and the Green Mountain Boys from Vermont. Yet now, the states of New York and New Jersey cannot cooperate on a simple bridge?"

"Won't get any argument from me. Though it isn't 'now,' it was sixty years ago." She shook her head. "Unfortunately, the damn bridge is falling apart."

Crane found himself squirming in the seat. "Is it safe to traverse it?"

"Not too many alternatives. Going down to the GWB's a bit much."

Neither sure what Mills meant by those initials, nor entirely sure he wished to know, he fell silent. They were almost back at Sleepy Hollow in any event.

Both Miss Jenny and Captain Irving were waiting for them at the armory. The latter regarded both of them with concern. "You two look like hell."

Mills burst out laughing. "You don't look so hot yourself, there, Captain."

"Yeah, well, you spend your day filing reports on cop-killings after being up all night."

Crane took a seat by the computing device. "That is, in fact, a fairly accurate précis of our day's toils as well, Captain."

"Though in our case, the cop was just wounded." Mills sat in the other chair.

The captain folded his arms. "At least you kept the cross out of the bad guys' hands. But we still don't know what they need it for."

"At least now we know *who*," Miss Jenny said.

"Serilda of Abaddon," Crane said solemnly. "She was responsible for a great deal of death and destruction."

"That was the Furth murder and that break-in, right?" Irving asked.

Mills nodded. "Crane encountered her back in the day, and her coven tried to resurrect her, but we put the kibosh on it."

Unbidden, the settlement near Albany that Serilda massacred came to the fore of Crane's mind. He recalled the sight of the smoky ruins of the tents, the smell of burnt flesh and rotten food—and the sound most of all because there was so little of it. The bodies were so badly burned that insects wouldn't even go near them, and the birdsong was unusually muted as well. He remembered standing there with General Washington and several others, and Washington commenting that he'd been expecting this since Trenton.

And then, suddenly, Crane rose to his feet. "Of course!"

"What?" Mills asked.

"The vision I received from Katrina. In addition to her verbal request for me to find my Congressional Cross, she showed me several visions from my past—including Serilda's massacre at Albany."

"Can I make a suggestion?" Miss Jenny asked the question while holding up a hand and pointing her index finger upward.

"By all means." Crane retook his seat.

"I think we need to look at the entire vision. It might help us figure out what the next step is, beyond making sure that the cross at the library doesn't get taken."

"About that," Irving said, "patrols and guards have reported nothing unusual. It's really quiet at the library this time of year anyhow, since it's between semesters."

Mills nodded. "That's good news, at least."

Crane closed his eyes for a moment, and recalled the vision he'd received in Patriots Park.

"First I was in a forest at night. There was a full moon. Then I found myself in different locations and times. The first was the van Brunt sitting room, where I was sharing a drink with Abraham."

Mills nodded. "He was one of the recipients of the medal, so that makes sense."

"Next was the Albany massacre by Serilda."

"The person responsible for this mess," Irving said.

"Not exactly," Mills said. "Like I said, we destroyed her bones. She's dead, and she can't come back. This is her followers with something up their sleeve."

"After that," Crane said, "I was in the Masonic cell where we captured Death and the late Lieutenant Brooks spoke as his voice."

"That was a fun night," Miss Jenny muttered.

Captain Irving said, "I'm not sure what that has to do with this."

"More hints, probably." Mills was rubbing her chin thoughtfully. "Remember, Brooks was the one who got the ball rolling on Serilda's attempt at resurrection, and van Brunt was Death."

Shuddering, the captain said, "I *hope* that's all it is. I really don't want to deal with *that* guy again."

"Nor I, Captain." Crane took a breath. "Next was the carnival where I was forced to kill the golem who was guarding my son."

Mills winced. "That doesn't seem to have anything to do with this."

Crane was about to agree when he recalled what the golem had done just before they found him. "Yes, it does. It is another hint regarding Serilda. During the war, it was Katrina's coven who cast the spell that weakened Serilda enough that she might be vulnerable to mortal attacks. She was burned at the stake, which only worked because of the coven's efforts."

Nodding, Mills said, "And before you killed the golem, the golem wiped out the remainder of the coven. All four of them."

"The point being that we will be unable to rely upon their assistance with this latest difficulty regarding Serilda's followers."

"So we're on our own." Mills shrugged. "What else is new?"

"What's the next vision you saw?" Irving asked.

"And can I just say that 'what's the next vision you saw' is just about the last question I ever expected to be asking anyone ever?"

Mills chuckled. "You and me both."

"We are all of us out of our depth, Captain," Crane said. "Prior to my first encounter with one of Moloch's minions when I was still in the service of the Crown, I too believed daemons and witches and spellcraft to be the stuff of legends and poetry. Yet here we are, encountering all three with alarming regularity. I believe that the time for astonishment is far in the past."

"Oh, trust me, I'm well aware of what we're dealing with and how real it is." Irving shook his head. "Just every once in a while I like to remind myself that this? Is *crazy*."

"Amen." Mills gave a brief bit of applause before turning to Crane. "So what was next?"

Crane shook his head. He didn't understand the value of such utterances as what Mills and Irving were indulging in. The reality of their lives was established. It was foolish to try to decry its sanity.

But he knew better than to try to argue with them on the subject. Besides, they had more pressing matters to contend with.

"The next vision was of Fort Carillon in Ticonderoga, a meeting that was held among myself, Caleb Whitcombe, and Henry Knox." He smirked. "I believe the lieutenant's and my recent journey to that town is all the explanation required for that particular experience."

Mills nodded. "Yeah. What was next?"

"The last vision before Katrina spoke to me was Marinus Willett leading a meeting of the Sons of Liberty in New York."

Irving frowned. "So we got Willett, Knox, van Brunt, and Whitcombe. But not Cortlandt or Tilghman. Why not?"

"The most simple explanation, Captain, is that I never met either gentleman in my travails during the war. Every one of the visions Katrina provided came from my own memory, after all."

"So what happened after that?" Mills asked.

Crane frowned. "I was back in the forest. Katrina appeared to me, spoke the words, 'You must retrieve the medal you were awarded!'"

"And the forest was the same as it was?"

"Yes, a darkened clearing surrounded by gnarled trees, and illuminated by the . . ." He trailed off. Everything Katrina had shown him in the vision had significance to what they were to accomplish against Serilda's coven. How much that was so had not really impinged on his consciousness until this conversation.

Which was why he didn't recall one particular detail until now. "At the start of the dream, the moon was full. But after the various visions concluded, and I was returned to the forest, it was a half-moon. And then right after Katrina's urging, there were *eight* half-moons."

"What?" That was Miss Jenny, who had been unusually quiet. Looking over, he saw that she was sitting in a corner of the room, a thick book with a cracked binding in her lap. "Eight half-moons? You sure?"

"Of course I'm sure. Why?"

Jenny got up, walked over to the table, and placed the book down. A considerable amount of dust flew into the air from the impact.

"Been reading up on this Serilda bitch. She led a cult that worshipped the demon Abaddon. Based on Corbin's notes, the cult's still active in Sleepy Hollow, which I guess you guys got a firsthand look at."

"Indeed," Crane said.

"Yeah," Mills added. "Go on."

"Well, the cult got really major around Christmas 1776."

Irving frowned. "Wasn't that when Washington crossed the Delaware?"

Crane nodded. "After being defeated in New York, the general led his troops to attack a Hessian regiment that occupied Trenton. It was a great victory."

Mills's eyes went wide. "Hessians? Those guys weren't just German mercs, though, they were Moloch's henchmen."

"Yes." Crane shook his head. "I didn't think

much of it at the time, but I do recall Washington saying in Albany, when we found the victims of Serilda's power, that he'd been afraid of such a happening since Trenton. His exact words were 'We both won and lost that day.'"

Jenny looked up at him. "My guess is that the Hessians at Trenton did something to make Serilda more than an average cult leader, and Washington didn't stop it in time."

"That would fit the pattern."

"But that's not the interesting part. Look at this." Jenny pointed at a passage in the book she'd placed on the table.

Crane bent over to peruse the page. "'The Witch Who is of Abaddon may be Destroyed, but fear not, for her Personage may be Resurrected at two times four the number of Half Moons following her Destruction.'" He looked up. "Eight half-moons."

"Oh crap." Mills was now holding her phone.

"What is it, Lieutenant?"

"I got a phases-of-the-moon app for my phone after the last time we went up against Serilda. I figured, given what we're dealing with, it's something I need to be up on."

Crane nodded. "It's true, magic is heavily influenced by lunar cycles."

"Right, so I just checked when the next half-moon is. It's tomorrow night—and tomorrow's half-moon is the eighth one since the blood moon on the night we destroyed Serilda's bones."

"Oh crap," Jenny said, echoing her sister's words. Crane wondered if it was a deliberate mocking of her sibling, or a signal of how alike the two were. "From what Al told me at the library, six of the Independence Crosses were used by Washington to stop Serilda's coven from killing his wife. I'm guessing that the runes that Mercier put on the side are a kind of—" Jenny faltered, struggling to find a word.

Crane ventured a term he'd learned in his all-too-brief experiences with the supernatural. "Necromancy? That *is* the study of death magic."

Jenny's mouth twisted a bit. "Not exactly. More like anti-necromancy. This *stops* death magic. Al said they were like spells of reinforcement or protection."

Irving put his hands on his hips. "So this is good, right?"

"Good, how?" Mills asked, sounding incredulous.

"They likely need six crosses. They've only got four, and after tomorrow night, they won't be any use to them anyhow."

"Assuming," Crane said, "that we are correct in our supposition."

Mills sighed. "Yeah, but it does fit the evidence, including what Stacy said before she died."

"We also cannot assume," Crane added, "that they only have four of the crosses. There are three unaccounted for by any means we have been able to track, but Serilda's coven has means beyond what we might imagine. They may have one of the three remaining crosses—including, quite possibly, my own."

Jenny said, "They may even have all three."

Mills shook her head. "No, if they did, they wouldn't have bothered going for the one in Ticonderoga. They need at least one more—and the only one left is sitting on Chestnut Street."

Crane moved toward the door. "Then I will hie myself there immediately, augment the protection you have so graciously provided, Captain, and perhaps question this Al to see if he can provide more enlightenment. Or, at the very least, provide me with more research materials."

"Good plan. I need to go home and get some sleep—remember, I got a ten a.m. court date."

Irving frowned. "Ippolito?"

Mills nodded. "After two four-hour drives in two days—not to mention that medieval torture device in the motel—I need eight hours in my own bed if I'm gonna be any good for Phil Czierniewski tomorrow."

"Of course. Sleep well, Lieutenant."

Irving joined them in their exodus toward the door. "I didn't even get anything as good as a medieval torture device. We'll confab in the morning."

They all stopped and turned back when they realized that Jenny hadn't joined them.

The younger Mills sister was smiling. "Well, I got a *great* night's sleep last night, and I didn't get up till ten, so I'm not even a little tired, and I'm gonna see if I can find anything else in Corbin's files. Now that I've got better info, I might be able to track more down."

"Excellent. Swift journeys, Miss Jenny," Crane said with a bow.

He departed, along with Irving and Mills. The two constables went to their vehicles. Crane walked, the crisp night air searing his lungs pleasantly. True, the cold was bitter, but it was nothing compared to the brutality of the conditions on the road from Ticonderoga to Boston. In addition, Crane didn't have to deal with the logistics of sixty pounds of cannon.

And, as he did in 1775 following the capture of Fort Carillon, he had a purpose. He would not allow Serilda's followers to again resurrect that witch.

ELEVEN

Sleepy Hollow, New York

JANUARY 2014

ALBERT JOHN WHITCOMBE-SEARS had always considered himself a rationalist and a skeptic. He believed only in what he could see with the evidence of his own eyes, or that which could be proven by scientific theory.

In this he was following in a family tradition. Both the Whitcombe family and the Sears family traced their lineage back to the first European colonists to come to the New World in the seventeenth and eighteenth centuries, and they were products of the Enlightenment. Since then, the tradition of both families was to only believe in the tangible.

What Al did not realize was that it also meant he'd find himself believing some things that seemed on their face to be impossible, yet he saw them with his own two eyes.

It was his first encounter with Sheriff August

Corbin that opened his eyes to what people referred to as the supernatural. Al never liked that term. If it occurred in the world, then it was natural. He found *supernatural* to be a contradiction in terms.

He still remembered the day when everything changed.

At the time, he'd been working as a reference librarian. He worked in the main reading room of what Al continued to insist was the New York Public Library's Research Building. It was referred to by the maps and tourist websites as the Stephen A. Schwarzman Building, thanks to Mr. Schwarzman's admittedly very generous donation of a hundred million dollars.

Regardless, he had commuted to Manhattan from his apartment in Sleepy Hollow five days a week for that job, while his father and uncle ran the Whitcombe-Sears Library, which had been in the family ever since the Episcopal Church gave up on the structure.

Then one day a decade ago, before Schwarzman's donation got the library named after him, Al got a call on his cell phone from a 914 number he didn't recognize. He almost didn't answer it. Most numbers he didn't have in his phone's directory turned out to be telemarketers, but it could've been one of the neighbors or some friend of the family whose number he hadn't put in the phone.

A gruff voice on the other end had said, "Mr. Whitcombe-Sears, this is Sheriff August Corbin in

Sleepy Hollow. I'm afraid I have some bad news. Your father and your uncle have been murdered."

Al no longer remembered any of the rest of the conversation. In fact, he no longer recalled anything that happened between his standing in the library's reading room with its high ceilings and susurrus of low-level noise made by people doing research and clacking on their laptops and hearing Corbin speaking the word *murdered,* and his standing outside the converted church next to Corbin in front of yellow crime-scene tape that blocked the entrance. Colored lights strobed in the air and he had asked Corbin, "What happened?"

"We're still trying to figure that out."

"Right." Al knew that was cop-speak for *we have no bloody clue what happened.* "I want to see the bodies."

"That's—that's not the best idea, Mr. Whitcombe-Sears."

"Why not?" Al had been indignant at the time that this tin-pot local cop would presume to tell him he couldn't see his own family's bodies.

After a hesitation, Corbin had said, "I'm okay with showing you your father, but not your uncle. I'm afraid that whatever did this—well, we only were able to identify your uncle because he still had his wallet and cell phone on him."

Corbin had taken him to see his father, who was in a body bag. Someone from the medical examiner's office unzipped it, and he saw his father with a shocked expression on his face and a very large hole in his chest.

"What did that?"

"We're not sure yet." Corbin had nodded to the other cop then, and zipped up the bag.

Al had gotten sick of that answer but said nothing.

It was that night that things got weird, as he had gone home to his apartment. He lived on the ground floor of a three-apartment townhouse. It had one bedroom, a small kitchen, and a large living room/dining room, plus access to the small backyard behind the townhouse. For obvious reasons, he had trouble sleeping that night. To make matters worse, his restless tossing and turning was interrupted by a tapping sound coming from the living room.

Padding out of his bedroom, he saw a figure standing on the other side of the sliding door to the backyard.

"Dad!?" He said the word before his sleepy mind realized what he was seeing.

His father was butt-naked, with the same big hole in his chest that he'd seen when he was in the body bag—dead!—and rapping on the window.

Unable to figure out what else to even do, Al went and slid the door open. "Dad, how—what—it—what're you *doing*?"

For a zombie, Dad had sounded remarkably coherent. "I'm sorry, son, but they're after me, and I've gotta hide."

"Dad, you're—you're *dead*."

"No one's more aware of that than me, son, believe me. Got a big hole in my chest and no pulse. Nonetheless, here I am, and there's some crazy guy after me. Chased me outta the morgue. Dunno how long I can give 'em the slip, but I needed somewhere to lie low, and the cops are at the house and the library."

Unable to bear the sight of his father like this—he honestly hadn't been sure what disturbed him more, the nudity or the aforementioned big hole—he had grabbed a bathrobe for his father to wear.

"I'm hoping that whoever that was trying to nab me won't think to look here. Even if they do, at least you can help me out."

"Uhm—*how* exactly?" Al had been grateful that he could now look at his father, though that mostly had just shown him how watery and yellow his father's eyes were now, and how sallow his skin.

"I've got no clue, son. It's my first time being dead."

Before Al could reply to that, the report of shattered glass filled his ears. Throwing his arms up to protect his face, he looked under his arms to see that something had smashed the sliding door from the outside, leaving shards of glass all over his living room floor.

To this day, Al couldn't adequately describe what he saw standing in the broken doorway. It was human-shaped, more or less, but he couldn't make out any features. It was like something he saw out of the corner of his eye—except it was like that when he was staring straight at it.

Its voice had been deep and resonant and sounded exactly what Al imagined death would sound like if it could talk. Though *talk* seemed an inadequate description for the sound that seemed to echo in Al's very bones.

You will come with me, Frederick Whitcombe-Sears. You have a task to perform.

"And what if I say no? You'll kill me?"

Al had to admit that he was impressed with his father's defiance in the face of—whatever this was.

I have already taken your brother. Shall I take your son as well?

"You're not taking anybody," said a gruff voice from the backyard.

Looking past the—the *thing*, Al had seen Corbin standing in the moonlight, pointing his pistol at the creature.

You are a fool, August Corbin, if you believe that your puny weapons of iron and steel can hurt me.

"Oh, you're right," Corbin had said. "Iron and steel? No chance. I'd be dead in a cold minute."

Then Corbin had pulled the trigger, which was even louder to Al than the breaking glass had been.

Right after the shot fired, the monster had screamed. He had seen the smoke emitting from the creature's—for lack of a better word—body, had smelled the stink of burning flesh, had heard the sizzling sound that the burning flesh made.

Corbin had squeezed the pistol's trigger a second time, and this time there had been another scream. The stink of burning flesh intensified to the point of nausea.

The creature had collapsed to the floor. Corbin had entered the apartment, stood over the monster, and then fired a third shot.

That third one had been the loudest of all. Al had feared that he would hear the echo of the third shot's report for the rest of his life. (He wouldn't. He often went weeks without thinking about it now, a decade later.)

He *knew*, though, that he'd recall the sight that followed until the day he died: the monster melted right there on his living room floor. The burned-flesh smell had gotten even worse, and Al had been convinced that the brown stain it was leaving on his tile floor would never ever come out. (It wouldn't. The landlord had to replace the floor, which came out of Al's security deposit.)

Al had just stared at Corbin, who smiled under his beard. "Silver bullets."

"That's it?" Al had been incredulous. "It's as simple as that to stop—whatever that thing is that turned my Dad into a zombie?"

"Not *that* simple—these things are impossible to find. Don't know how the Lone Ranger managed it."

"Sheriff, what's—" Al had started to say, but he had been cut off by a plaintive moan from behind him.

"Ooooooh, boy."

Whirling around, Al had seen his father collapse onto the living room floor right next to the—the whatever it was.

"Dad!" Al had run to his father's side as he had collapsed, but he no longer moved or spoke or did anything. Kneeling down beside him, Al had checked for a pulse—but, of course, that yielded no useful results, since he hadn't had a pulse when he was walking around a moment ago, either.

Corbin had put a hand on his shoulder. "I'm sorry, Mr. Whitcombe-Sears. But your father is really dead. This demon here brought him back to life long enough to try to get a book out of that library of his."

Al had looked at Corbin incredulously then. "All this for a book? And what do you mean, 'demon'? There's no such thing!" Before Corbin could say anything in reply, Al had then said, "And there's no such thing as zombies, either, says the guy who just had a conversation with his dead father. I still don't understand any of this, though."

"Let me take care of this mess first. I'll get your father's body back to the morgue, then I'll get a hazmat team in here to clean up the mess. You free for lunch tomorrow?"

Al had looked around helplessly. "I really don't think I'm going to work, so yeah, I'm free for lunch."

"Meet me at McCabe's tomorrow at twelve thirty. You ever been to McCabe's?"

Al had just shaken his head.

"Best apple pie à la mode you've ever had."

Corbin had been as good as his word. Dad's body was returned to the morgue without any official report, and a hazmat team did the best they could with his floor, though it wasn't enough to get rid of the brown stain of whatever it was.

The next day, he did indeed meet Corbin for lunch at McCabe's.

"I was like you, once," Corbin had said. "I thought that monsters were stories. But they're not. They're real, they exist, and one of them mutilated your uncle and then killed your father and turned him into a zombie."

"This is—a lot to process."

"I don't doubt it."

"How'd you know to use silver bullets?"

Corbin had scooped up some of the vanilla ice cream that surrounded his apple pie. "I didn't, at first. In stories, monsters would often be vulnerable to silver bullets, so I took a shot." He had smiled, then, and added, "So to speak," then had popped the ice cream into his mouth. "Anyway, it worked the first time, and I had to hope it would work this time, too."

Al had inherited the library, and so he gave his notice to NYPL and then took over the family business. He found a number of fascinating texts in the rare-books section of the library—kept up near where the church organ used to be—including one text that informed him that the demon who killed Dad and Uncle Charlie was named Uzobach.

Corbin would continue to call upon him for research, later sending along his protégé Jenny Mills.

But now, all hell was breaking loose. The first of the Horsemen of the Apocalypse had arrived, the two Witnesses (one of whom was Corbin's partner, Jenny's sister Abbie) had begun their work, Corbin was beheaded, and Al was frightened.

He didn't believe in prophecy. Or, more to the point, he didn't believe that prophecies had to come true. Knowing the future automatically changes it, and Al didn't believe for a second that *anything* was preordained.

Still, he was frightened, mostly because Corbin was dead. Jenny was a good kid, but sometimes was a little crazy. Not the kind of crazy they stuck her in Tarrytown Psychiatric for, but still. And Corbin had limited the people who knew the truth to those who encountered it first. So Al was part of the "inner circle" thanks to what happened with his father, and Jenny was because she was possessed by a less substantial demon than Uzobach.

But Abbie Mills wasn't, and now she was at the vanguard of this whole nonsense, along with a time-displaced Revolutionary War soldier, something Al—even with everything he'd seen—wouldn't have believed if Jenny hadn't insisted. She'd told him the whole story after Al had told her about how Washington used the Independence Crosses.

Al also realized that he couldn't remember the guy's name. It was something vaguely birdlike, but that was all he could recall.

He was sitting in the library going through some old tomes, trying to find out more about Mercier the silversmith.

"Eureka!" he cried out when he finally found what he was looking for in a text by a nineteenth-century mesmerist named Lawrence Conroy, who had been associated with Aleister Crowley, and who had been targeted by Harry Houdini. The famous magician had made an aggressive hobby of debunking the many frauds who peddled magic and spiritualism.

As it happened, Houdini never was able to debunk Conroy, and Al knew why: he was a legitimate student of magic, and he knew everything there was to know about the runes used by the great alchemist Gaston Mercier.

One of the two officers who'd been assigned to guard the library against the theft of their Congressional Cross wandered by the desk, just as Al finished reading up on the runes and how they might be used on items of spiritual significance that were made of silver—like, say, the Independence Crosses.

"Hey, Al, me and Diana are gonna order from the Chinese place. You want anything?"

"Some fried dumplings would be good, thanks, Ray." Then a thought occurred. "Hey, Ray, that British guy who's consulting on Corbin's murder. What's his name again?"

"Ichabod Crane, why?"

"Really?"

"Yeah I know, but hey, I've gone through life with the last name Drosopoulos, so who am I to judge?"

Al smiled, in part because he got the bird part right, but mostly because he knew that name.

"I gotta check something downstairs."

"Okay. We'll let you know when the food gets here."

Nodding, Al went to the back, past the exhibits and downstairs. In addition to the restrooms, the library's basement also served as storage for the exhibits that were not on display.

Al spent the better part of half an hour digging around trying and failing to find what he was looking for. He might not have taken so long if he didn't keep getting distracted by shiny things—sometimes literally, as the collection included a lot of jewelry. He'd been the caretaker of the library for ten years now, and he'd acquired a few pieces on his own, but there were still a lot of things that Dad and Uncle Charlie, not to mention Grandma before them, had collected that Al hadn't yet catalogued. He'd been meaning to get around to it, but cataloguing had always been Al's least favorite part of librarianship.

Serving the public, he loved. There were few things more satisfying than helping someone find what they need, especially when it was clear when they arrived at the desk that *they* didn't even know what that was, at first, until Al helped them get there.

Putting the exhibits together was also fun—finding all the wonderful treasures that he and his family had accumulated over the decades and finding the right combination of them to make for a particularly fine display . . .

He even liked shelving, which was usually the top of the list of library workers' least favorite tasks. The act of putting a book away in the right place so it could be found again by the next person who'd need it gave him a huge sense of accomplishment for some reason.

But he hated cataloguing. A tendency he was regretting at this particular instant, since if he had catalogued it all, he'd know where to find the stupid thing.

It was right when he found it that he heard Diana's voice from upstairs. "Yo, Al, food's here!"

"Be right up!" he called up the stairs. The item had been wrapped in cloth and stored in a small wooden box that was slightly warped. But then, the box in question was more than two centuries old.

He set the item, still cradled in the cloth that

it had been wrapped in, aside on top of one of the crates.

As he hopped up the stairs, taking them two at a time—suddenly, he was really hungry—he heard a horrible scream from upstairs.

He hesitated, stumbling on the top step and almost falling back down them. Reaching out, he snagged the railing with his right hand, and managed to right himself, but his wrist twisted in an odd direction.

Wincing with pain, he cradled his right hand in his left arm and continued up the stairs more slowly.

The last time he heard a scream like that, it was when Corbin's silver bullets had struck the flesh of the demon Uzobach.

"Diana? Ray? You guys okay?"

Silence greeted his request.

Throwing common sense to the wind, he left the staircase and slowly worked his way to the doorway that led to the main part of the library.

He saw nothing except for the main desk, the computer stations, and the many shelves of books. He heard nothing except for the low hum of the computers and that annoying flickering buzz that one of the fluorescent lights always made no matter how many times he changed the bulb.

Slowly, he moved into the library. "Hello?"

Reaching into his pocket, he fumbled for his cell phone. He took it out, pushed the button on top—and nothing happened. He winced, remembering that he'd intended to stick it in the charger an hour ago, and then never did.

There was a phone on the main desk. Just about thirty feet away. All he had to do was get to that and call 911, because there was no way Ray and Diana would just go quiet like this.

That was when he realized that he couldn't even hear the squawk of either cop's radio, which had been a pretty constant noise the past day. He'd gotten so used to it, he didn't notice it anymore, but now it was conspicuous by its absence. And Diana had only told him to come upstairs a few seconds before. What could have happened to her in so short a time?

That he had about half a dozen answers to his rhetorical question off the top of his head did not make him feel any safer, or any less exposed as he slowly made his way to his desk.

He reached his desk, and started to grab for the phone when he saw the bodies.

Prior to tonight, Al would have said that the experience of seeing his father with a huge hole in his chest—and then later seeing him walking around despite still having the selfsame hole—would have inured him to seeing dead bodies.

He was incredibly wrong.

Corbin had told him he didn't want to see what the demon did to Uncle Charlie, and he was finally starting to get what the sheriff had been talking about. Because lying in the center aisle between the bookcases were two torsos, four arms, four legs, and two heads.

The body parts were strewn haphazardly about the aisle, but the heads of Officers Ray Drosopoulos and Diana Han were positioned so that their dead eyes and open bloody mouths were staring right at the desk.

Al was all set to bend over and throw up when he felt a very long, very cold piece of metal impale him in the back.

From behind him, a voice said, "Sorry, but I'm afraid I need your blood."

WHEN CRANE ENTERED the Whitcombe-Sears Library, his nose was immediately assaulted by an all-too-familiar smell.

It was one that often invaded his nostrils on the battlefield, and had done so again most recently at the Cortlandt Museum.

The smell of death.

At first, he hadn't encountered it much. Initially, his time both as a redcoat and as part of the Continental Army was mercifully free of the appallingly high body counts that some of his fellows had dealt with.

But then he found the settlement outside Albany that Serilda had destroyed. The sheer number of bodies was overwhelming, and the stench was just *awful*. Over the years, he would encounter death more times than he could count—including his own—and he had yet to wholly get used to it.

Were he lucky, he never would.

Now he found himself confronted with another charnel house, this in the passageway between rows of bookcases. He found another massacre very much like the one in the Tarrytown museum. This time it appeared to be two of Irving's subordinates in the local constabulary.

Then he heard a moan from behind the desk, which was located at the far end of the space— where the altar would have been when this struc- ture had served as a house of worship.

Gingerly moving past the torn-apart bodies of the two officers, he worked his way back to find a man with receding gray and white hair, lying on the floor behind the desk in an ever-increasing pool of blood.

"Damn." Crane ran to him and tried to see how bad it was.

"Call . . . help . . ."

Crane cursed himself for a fool, and immediately fumbled for his cell phone. He recalled that via the simple expedient of dialing the number nine fol- lowed by one twice, he could summon police, fire brigade, and physicians, all at the same time.

Two of those three were needed now.

"Nine-one-one, please state your emergency."

"I'm at the Whitcombe-Sears Library in Sleepy Hollow—there are two murdered constables, and the proprietor of the library has been badly wounded. He has lost considerable amounts of blood."

"All right, sir, stay there, please. Emergency medical technicians and the police are on their way."

"Thank you very kindly, madam."

"Crane . . ."

Looking over in surprise at the prone form next to him, Crane absently dropped the phone and said, "You have the advantage of me, sir, though I assume you're Albert Whitcombe-Sears."

Whitcombe-Sears nodded. "I—I have something that—that belongs to you. . . ."

"I—I don't—"

"Downstairs . . . Storage room . . . On top of one of the crates, there's anoth—another Congressional Cross. . . . It's—it's yours."

Crane's eyes went wide. "What?"

"Your—your cross . . . My—my family had it, since no one—no one could find any—any heirs to give it—it to. . . ."

"I will retrieve it shortly, sir. Please, do save your breath. The ambulance will arrive shortly, and—"

Then Whitcombe-Sears grabbed Crane's right arm with an iron grip formed by his left hand. After the initial grab, though, the man's strength weakened.

"They will try—try to resurrect Serilda with the blood of—blood of a descendant of one of the—the recipients of—of the cross. . . ."

Crane frowned. "I thought Washington was able to cast away death without any blood being used."

"Blood—strengthens the spell . . . Connection to—to recipients stronger with time . . . Said they needed my blood when they stabbed me, so coven using—using *my* blood to strengthen *their* spell . . . You—you must cast the counterspell with—with one cross and the blood of its recipient. . . ." He managed to lift his right arm and point to the main desk. "There's a—a *grimoire* on the desk. . . . Found it when I was—I was researching Mercier. Take it—it has the counterspell. . . ." His left hand's grip on Crane's arm strengthened, and Whitcombe-Sears tried to sit up. "Only *you* can do it! *No one* else!"

And then Albert Whitcombe-Sears coughed once and slumped to the floor. His left hand's grip completely loosened on Crane's arm.

The man was dead.

"*Requiescat in pace*, Mr. Whitcombe-Sears," Crane whispered. Then he clambered to his feet, cursing himself for not arriving sooner.

For a moment, he just stared at the body of the man whose ancestor was a trusted comrade. Though Knox led the expedition, Whitcombe's contribution was incalculable, and the cannon would never have reached Boston without him. Crane shuddered to think how the war would have proceeded had they not taken Boston in the spring of 1776.

Crane imagined that his friend would have been

proud to see what a good man his descendant was. And been as outraged as Crane was now at the manner of his death.

Then he lifted his head, a new smell overlaying the miasma of death that permeated the converted church.

It was, he realized, smoke.

Looking down the aisle of the library, he saw that one of the bookcases was alight. Only moments later, two more bookcases were on fire, and Crane knew he no longer had much time. Wooden bookcases filled with paper books would be nothing more than fuel for an ever-mounting fire.

Only then did he hear the weak voice over his cell phone, which was still on the floor. "Sir? Are you still there?"

He snagged the phone. "Yes, and I'm afraid you'll need to send the fire brigade as well. Someone has set the library alight!"

"The ambulance is moments away, sir—I'm summoning the Sleepy Hollow Fire Department now."

"My thanks, madam. Now if you will forgive me, I have a critical errand to run."

Pocketing the phone in his coat and grabbing the *grimoire* that Whitcombe-Sears had indicated, he ran to the back room where Miss Jenny had said the exhibits were.

Not at all unexpectedly, the case with the Congressional Cross that had been issued to Caleb Whitcombe was opened, the cross itself gone.

Turning, he tucked the *grimoire* inside his shirt to protect it from the smoke and fire and to keep his hands free. The leather binding rubbed uncomfortably against his skin as he dashed to the staircase leading downward. He hoped the storage room that Whitcombe-Sears mentioned was easy to find.

It was, and it didn't take him long to spy a small item wrapped in cloth. Grabbing for it eagerly, Crane unwrapped the cloth to find a cross that looked just like the one in Ticonderoga and the ones he saw photographs of on the computing machine.

For a moment, he just stared at it. He recalled receiving notification of his receipt of the Congressional Cross. It was, in fact, right after the very meeting of the Sons of Liberty that he and van Brunt had attended—the same meeting Katrina had shown him in a vision. A messenger had arrived at the small inn on Gold Street in New York where the meeting had taken place.

"Excuse me," the man had said. He had been covered in grime, and had smelled of salt water, indicating to Crane that he had come to Manhattan within the last few hours by boat or ferry. "Do I have the pleasure of addressing Mr. Willett of New York?"

"You do," Willett had said in reply.

The messenger had then turned to Crane and van Brunt. "And might you two gentlemen be, or have knowledge of, Mr. Crane of Oxford and Mr. van Brunt, also of New York?"

"We are those gentlemen," van Brunt had said in reply.

"Excellent. I have come from the Congress in Philadelphia with instructions to find you three. I thought fortune had favored me when I was told that you two sirs"—he had looked at Crane and van Brunt—"were scheduled to attend a Sons of Liberty meeting to be led by you, sir." He had then looked at Willett.

"Fortune has indeed favored you," Willett had said. "What news from the Congress?"

"They have appointed Mr. Washington of Virginia as the commanding general of the army."

Willett had nodded. "An excellent choice."

Crane, however, had frowned. His switching sides at the urging of van Brunt's fiancée Katrina van Tassel was relatively recent. "I do not know the man."

"He is," van Brunt had said, "a gentleman of the highest order, and a great leader. He could command men to walk into fire, and all they'd ask is if they should leave their boots on. The Congress has chosen well."

The messenger had gone on. "At Mr. Washington's—pardon, at *General* Washington's request, the Congress has also awarded ten men with the Congressional Cross, in honor of great achievement in the attempt to gain liberty for the colonies. Three of those ten men are from New

York, and it is my privilege to provide you each with official notification of your honors."

At that point, the man had reached into the pouch that had been slung across his shoulder, and presented each of them with a rolled-up scroll secured with the wax seal of the Continental Congress.

Crane had broken the seal and unfurled his scroll. With a small smile, he had said, "You described this as a 'cross,' did you not?" He had held the scroll up for the messenger to inspect. "I was unaware that crosses were made of parchment."

Chuckling, the messenger had said, "The Congress has commissioned a French silversmith known to General Washington to fashion the crosses. Upon their completion, they will be delivered to you. God willing, we will have at last resolved our conflict with the Crown by then."

"Let us hope," Willett had said.

Now, almost 239 years later, Crane finally held the cross in his hand. And based on what Whitcombe-Sears had said, his holding this cross that had been earmarked for him was, as Katrina had indicated by her urgent request for him to find it, the only way to stop Serilda from once again rising.

A roar from upstairs reminded him that he would not be preventing anything if he did not remove himself from the premises posthaste.

He felt a blast of heat as he mounted the staircase, and winced when he entered the main section of the library and saw that most of the bookcases were consumed by massive flames.

There were many things that Ichabod Crane believed in that had been proven false over the last few subjective years. When he enlisted in the Regular Army, he believed that the colonists were upstarts who needed to be taught a lesson. When he interrogated the prisoner Arthur Bernard under orders from Colonel Tarleton, he believed that daemons and monsters were the stuff of superstitious legend that had no place in an enlightened society—a belief shattered when Tarleton revealed himself to be such a daemon right after he murdered Bernard. When the Horseman's broad axe mortally wounded Crane, he believed that he was dead.

He also believed that his wife was not a witch and that he and Katrina had no children.

All those beliefs were shattered in due course, and so many more had been demolished since his unexpected resurrection that he scarcely knew why he chose to believe in anything.

But one thing he had held on to was his scholar's certainty that the one thing that separated humanity from the beasts of the field was the accumulation of knowledge.

And so to see so much knowledge go up in flames was the latest in a series of heartbreaking occurrences. He had been a history professor before his patriotism got the better of him and he left Oxford to enlist, thus setting him inexorably on the path that led to him standing in a burning building almost three centuries after his birth.

The sound of the Klaxons used by police and fire vehicles broke him out of his reverie. He looked around, trying in vain to ascertain a way out of the library. He faced a wall of flame that served as an effective barricade to the front entrance. Even the aisle was alight, the mutilated remains of the two officers now also burning.

Recalling that there was a metal door visible at the far end of the corridor that also adjoined the staircase and the exhibit hall, Crane went back the way he came.

But just as he approached the large doorway, the massive wooden door that was propped open suddenly whirled around and slammed shut.

Another of Crane's beliefs that had been destroyed was the surety that doors did not close without a human hand or a mechanism acting upon it.

An unearthly voice echoed over the flames and the ever-louder Klaxons. *You will not be permitted to escape, Ichabod Crane. Like the fool who ran this library, your time is over.*

Defiantly, Crane looked up, shaking a fist in the air. "My time has been 'over' on many occasions, yet I am still here! I have survived many battles on this plane and the next! I have imprisoned Death! Do not imagine, then, that I am helpless before your sorcery!"

Even as he bellowed, a portion of the balcony at the front end of the library started to visibly buckle, its collapse imminent.

Turning, and trying to ignore the tickle in his throat, Crane grabbed for the metal pull-handle on the wooden door that had been magically shut, then pulled his hand away quickly. It was white-hot to the touch. Crane wasn't sure if the heat came from the fire or the eldritch machinations of Serilda's follower, and it ultimately didn't matter.

The Klaxons had steadied in their volume, meaning they were as close as they could be. Distantly, Crane could make out the sounds of water rushing, and he assumed that the fire brigade were beginning their work.

However, the tickle in his throat was building to a full-on cough. Glancing around, he noticed that, while most of the accoutrements of the structure's former function as a church had been removed, the lectern was still present. It was a simple wooden podium. A quick examination revealed that it was in two parts, with a short upper portion that latched on to the much longer lower portion. Crane assumed the top part was there to allow for taller ministers, and its ability to be removed to accommodate the shorter ones.

Either way, it was the best weapon Crane had

available. As he unlatched the top portion, Crane was extremely grateful that this hadn't been a Catholic house of worship. The lecterns in those churches tended toward the ornate, and taking off a piece of that while in a burning building would likely have been impossible.

The door that had slammed looked as though it was made of oak, so Crane didn't even bother trying that. Instead, he slowly worked his way along the side wall, keeping his eyes firmly on the roaring flames, and periodically pausing to cough so violently, he felt it in his ribs, until he reached a window.

Again, he was grateful that this place wasn't Catholic originally. Crane would have hated to have damaged a stained glass window.

Hefting the lectern portion over his head, he then swung the large block of wood around his body and threw it at the window, throwing himself to the floor as he did so.

The glass shattered over his head, though he barely heard that noise over the flames, the Klaxons, and the water, which, he hoped, was at least tamping down the flames on *some* part of the structure. As soon as the lectern went through the window, the flames were drawn to the outside. Crane felt the heat on his head and hair.

His first night in the twenty-first century, Crane had found himself, following Sheriff Corbin's murder, surrounded by lights of many colors that flickered and awful Klaxons, and dozens of men—and women, which had surprised him at the time—in uniform. The assault on his senses was overwhelming, and it was the most frightening experience of Crane's life. Given what he had seen during the war, that was not a light claim, but a true one, nonetheless.

Tonight, as he stumbled toward Chestnut Street after climbing out of the window that he'd broken, that selfsame sight of vehicles belonging to the police and the fire brigade, the Klaxons, and the people in uniform was the most welcoming sight he could imagine.

Even more welcome was the voice that cried out, "Crane!"

More coughs spasmed Crane's body, preventing him from answering Lieutenant Mills directly, but she came to him and guided him the rest of the way toward a third type of vehicle that he hadn't noticed at first: an ambulance.

As she led him over, Crane, still coughing, reached into the space between his shirt and his chest and pulled out Whitcombe-Sears's *grimoire*. "Guard this," he managed to get out between coughs.

"You got it," Mills said, trusting him unconditionally. Grateful, Crane allowed himself to be put in the hands of one of the medical technicians.

TWELVE

White Plains, New York

JANUARY 2014

ABBIE MILLS WAS finishing her third cup of coffee when she pulled into the parking garage that serviced the Westchester Supreme and County Court on Dr. Martin Luther King Jr. Boulevard in White Plains. On the one hand, she resented that testifying in the Ippolito case was cutting into her ability to sleep in. The last forty-eight hours had included eight hours of driving, two crappy nights' sleep, and yet another Crane crisis, complete with violence, magic, death, and history all rolled into one insane package. Worse, two of the deaths in question were Officers Drosopoulos and Han, two good people who deserved better than to be carved to bits by one of Serilda's coven.

On the other hand, she really relished the idea of doing something so banal as testifying in a criminal trial. It reminded her of when she used to be a cop rather than a Witness.

Not that she wasn't a cop, still, but she did so little casework lately, it was starting to frustrate her. Sure, there wasn't much paperwork involved in helping Crane avert the apocalypse, but there also wasn't much police work.

The Abbie Mills who arrested Johnny Ippolito eighteen months ago would have dreaded testifying in the resultant trial. However, the present-day Abbie Mills, who had spent the last several months being attacked by witches, golems, demons, animated trees, and one of the Horsemen of the Apocalypse, was seriously looking forward to the repetitive tedium of a cross-examination under oath.

When she went into the courthouse from the garage, she saw Phil Czierniewski waiting for her in the hallway. The tall, gangly lawyer was pacing like an expectant father, the fluorescent lights reflecting off his bald pate. As soon as he saw Abbie, he stopped, faced her, and clapped his hands the way he did.

Frowning, she asked, "Why aren't you in the courtroom?"

"Judge Olesen had a family thing, so we're not starting until noon."

Abbie rolled her eyes. "Y'know, Phil, we have this amazing piece of technology called a cell phone. I know you know about it, 'cause you've been using it to crawl up my butt about this testimony for the last week."

"I know, but—"

"Do you know how much I wanted to sleep in today?"

Phil waved his hands back and forth in front of his face. "*If* you'll let me get a word in?"

Putting her hands on her hips, Abbie just stared at the prosecutor.

"I didn't call you because Ippolito wants to make a deal."

"You have *got* to be kidding me. *Now* he wants to make a deal?"

Phil pointed a bony finger at her. "Specifically, he wants to make a deal with *you*. Says he's got something for one of your current cases."

Abbie's arms dropped to her sides. "Excuse me?"

"That's what he said." Phil shrugged. "What's the big deal?"

"I've only got one case right now, and there's no *way* Ippolito's involved in it." She shook her head. "Least I hope not. All right, where is he?"

"With his lawyer in one of the meeting rooms. Just waiting for you." Phil turned and started to lope down the hallway.

"Hang on, I am *not* doing this without more coffee." She went to the vending machine that was just down the hall and inserted a dollar bill, which provided her with a tiny cup filled with some of the worst coffee she'd ever had in her life.

Once the coffee was obtained and she'd sipped enough of the liquid cardboard that it wouldn't spill as she endeavored to keep up with Phil's longer gait, they soon reached their destination.

The meeting room was one of several set aside in the courthouse for occasions such as this: lawyer consultation, deal making, witness prep, and so on. A rectangular metal desk sat in the middle of the room, with six uncomfortable metal chairs around it, two on each long side and one each at the shorter sides. The walls were all industrial brickwork painted a sickly off-white.

Johnny Ippolito was in his prison oranges practically bouncing in his chair. Like Phil, he was bald, but unlike Phil—who'd shaved his monk's fringe to go for the fully smooth-headed look—Ippolito had the lamest of lame comb-overs.

Next to him was his ambulance-chaser lawyer David Petersen, a short, mousy guy in an Armani suit. The only thing Abbie disliked about baseball season was seeing his mug on the cheesy ads that he ran on local stations like SNY, which broadcast Mets games.

"Good, good, good, y'here." Ippolito indicated the chair opposite him. "Have a seat, Lieutenant, I got somethin' for ya."

Abbie sat in the indicated chair, trying not to squirm as it began to do its usual number on her back. She placed the coffee on the table. Phil took the seat next to her.

"Phil tells me that you've got something relating to my current case?"

"That's—"

Petersen put a hand on Ippolito's shoulder. "Now hold on a moment, please, John. Lieutenant Mills, Mr. Czierniewski: you and I both know that my client won't say a word until I have certain assurances."

Rolling her eyes, Abbie said, "Oh, *please*."

"That attitude, Lieutenant, will get you nowhere."

"I can say the same to you, Mr. Petersen. We aren't giving out assurances today. Best your client can hope for"—she turned her gaze upon Ippolito—"is a consideration."

"Excuse me, Lieutenant, but I believe you're speaking out of turn." The lawyer turned his bespectacled gaze upon Phil. "The assistant district attorney is the man empowered to speak here."

Phil smiled. Abbie had never liked Phil's smile, as it always looked like the expression a shark would get before it chowed down on a bunch of tiny, defenseless fish, but she had to admit that it worked nicely across this particular table.

"Mr. Petersen, the only reason we're having this meeting is because Judge Olesen had an emergency. Lieutenant Mills is here to provide testimony that's going to combine with the sworn statement made by the late Sheriff Corbin—a very beloved figure in the community who was tragically killed only a few short months ago—to put your client away for several years. You've had plenty of time to make a deal before this, and this eleventh-hour play isn't impressing me. Also? Your client requested Lieutenant Mills by name. So I'm inclined to follow her lead on this." He leaned back and gave Abbie a *you're on* look.

Smiling sweetly, Abbie said, "Okay, Ippolito. Try to impress *me*."

"All right, look, I *know* stuff, okay? I got people 'at talk t'me all'a time. I don't even wanna know about half this crap, but they tell me anyhow. I mean, it's a small community, y'know what I'm sayin'?"

Abbie started drumming her fingers on the metal table. It echoed off the walls. Reaching for the awful coffee, she said, "Ippolito, seriously, you *are* gonna come to the point before I take another sip of this sludge, or the rest of it goes down your jumpsuit."

Ippolito held up both hands. "Okay, okay, okay, fine, the point." He took a breath. "See, I heard some things 'bout a guy I know. He's a guy who knows stuff about stuff, y'know?"

"What *kind* of stuff?" Abbie was now holding the coffee menacingly near her mouth.

"Security plans, okay? For museums, and stuff."

Abbie put down the coffee. "Which museums?"

Petersen chose this moment to put himself back in the conversation. "Obviously, this *does* pertain to your current case, Lieutenant, so—"

While still looking at Ippolito, Abbie held up a

finger in the direction of the lawyer. "Mr. Petersen, I can just as easily pour coffee down *your* shirt."

Sputtering, Petersen said, "How dare you—"

"Oh, cut that out, David," Phil said, "I know what your hourly rate is, you can afford a new suit."

Abbie maintained her most intense *don't screw with me* stare on Ippolito. "Which museums?"

"The Museum'a the City'a New York, the Cortlandt Museum, an' the Whitcombe-Sears Library."

Again Abbie maintained her poker face, even though she was jumping cartwheels internally. "Yeah, and?"

"Whaddaya mean, 'yeah, and'? This is good stuff!" Ippolito was now flailing about in his chair.

"Right now, it's just you naming three museums and talking about some guy. None of this is helping me out much."

"All right, all right, all right, all right." Ippolito waved his hands back and forth at the wrist. "You want a name? I can give you a name."

"Which name?"

Ippolito frowned. "Whaddaya mean which name?"

"I mean," Abbie said, trying to keep her patience intact, "the name of the friend of yours or the name of the person who *hired* the friend of yours. And for the record? The second name would be a *lot* more useful to me."

Before Ippolito could say anything, Petersen pounced. "How much more useful?"

Abbie threw a quick glance at Phil, who just shrugged. He'd already said he'd follow her lead.

"You give me the person who hired your friend, I think that ADA Czierniewski could be convinced to move for dismissal when Judge Olesen finally shows up."

"Excellent." Petersen turned to Ippolito. "Tell her."

Ippolito, though, now looked like he'd swallowed something that made him nauseous. "That's kinda gonna be a little teeny-tiny bit of a problem."

Abbie just stared at him.

"Don't look at me like that, I *hate* when you look at me like that." Ippolito turned away, started staring at the ceiling. "Look, I ain't got *that* name. I just got the name of the guy I know. *Him* I can give you, no problem. But I dunno who hired him."

Turning to Phil, Abbie said, "That's not really worth a dismissal, is it?"

Phil shook his head. "No, but I'd be willing to cut a deal for time served in exchange for that name—assuming it's actually useful to Lieutenant Mills." He added that last with a conciliatory gesture to Abbie.

The fact was, it would be useful to Abbie no matter what, as the person who checked security for these robberies was the first real lead they had on who did this, beyond "members of Serilda's coven," which wasn't something she could enter into the database at headquarters.

But if she had someone to lean on? That was something she could work with—a thread she could pull.

"So to be clear," Petersen said, one arm on Ippolito's shoulder as if trying to hold him down in case he flew off, "if my client provides you with this intelligence, you promise to ask the judge for time served in exchange for a guilty plea?"

Phil nodded. "I can have it written up for you by the time Judge Olesen finally makes it in."

Petersen leaned back. "Then sit tight, because we're not giving up anything until I see that document."

Phil unfolded himself into an upright position and pulled out his phone. "I'll make the call now."

For several seconds, Abbie stared at Ippolito, who fidgeted in his chair. "Can I ask you something?" she finally asked.

"Knock yourself out."

"You've been sitting in lockup for eighteen months. Corbin and I offered you a plea deal way back when. You could've plead guilty to trespassing, and you'd have already served your time."

"Nah. Nah, nah, nah." Ippolito shook his head so fast Abbie feared it would start spinning around. "Can't do that. I didn't trespass, I broke an' I entered. If my record—if the *official record* of the United States says that I'm guilty'a somethin', then dammit, it's gonna say that I'm guilty'a somethin' I actually *did*. None'a this trespassin' crap. I got scruples, y'know."

Abbie rolled her eyes. "Ippolito, you can't even spell *scruples*."

"Sure I can! S-K-R-U—"

"I rest my case."

Now Ippolito was frowning. "Wait—is it S-K-R-O-O—"

"So if you didn't want to plead down, why didn't you give me something like this sooner?"

He shrugged. "Didn't have nothin' till today from somebody who was talkin' inside. Like I said, scruples. However the hell you spell it."

WITHIN AN HOUR, Phil had a plea agreement, which Ippolito signed, and then Abbie had a name, Carl Polchinski, and three addresses, none of which were actually his.

"Y'see," Ippolito had said, "Polchinski is a couch surfer. Sometimes with his mom, sometimes with his girlfriend, sometimes with his sister. Basically, whichever one's the least pissed-off at him, that's who he's stayin' with."

She called Crane's cell first. "Good morning, Lieutenant. Is your testimony complete?"

"Not exactly. Ippolito gave me the name of someone who was hired to check the security for all three local places that had Independence Crosses taken."

Crane said, "But Lieutenant—four locations were burglarized. Besides the museum in Tarrytown and the library here in Sleepy Hollow, there were *two* museums within the city of New York that were burglarized."

Abbie frowned. She had forgotten about the Metropolitan Museum, which had started this whole ball rolling, along with Crane's vision. "Well, I'm gonna have this guy picked up and see what he says."

"Excellent. I'd offer to join you, but I'm currently struggling with the *grimoire* that the late Mr. Whitcombe-Sears provided."

Not liking the sound of that, Abbie asked, "Struggling why?"

"He informed me before he expired that there was a spell to thwart the resurrection of Serilda this night in this *grimoire*. However, he neglected to inform me *which* of the two hundred pages of faded Latin text contains the spell."

"Lucky you. Well, you stick with that, then. I'll keep you posted."

Her next call was to headquarters. Detective Jones answered, and she gave him the name, the connection to the break-ins and murders at the Cortlandt Museum and the Whitcombe-Sears Library, and the three addresses Ippolito had provided.

"Uhm," Jones said, "I can send uniforms to the two places here in town, but the mother's place is in Tarrytown."

Abbie winced. Technically, the Cortlandt Museum thing was Detective Costa's case. "You take care of those two, I'll call Costa in Tarrytown."

Jones snorted. "Better you than me."

After ending the call with Jones, Abbie dialed the main number for Tarrytown PD. Costa wasn't at her desk, but she was home, and the sergeant gave her the detective's cell phone number

She answered on the first ring. "What do you want, Mills?"

"Good to hear your voice, Costa. I got a break in a case we share."

"Since when do we share a case?"

Abbie ground her teeth at Costa's acerbic tone. "Since about five minutes ago. You know that fire at the Whitcombe-Sears Library?"

Costa's tone, to Abbie's relief, softened. "I heard about that. Sorry about Han and Drosopoulos."

"Thanks." Abbie blew out a breath. "I just got a tip from a CI who's very much in the B-and-E community that a guy was hired to learn about the security of both the Cortlandt and Whitcombe-Sears—as well as the Museum of the City of New York."

"Didn't they get hit with a B-and-E/murder combo, too?"

Even though it was lost over the phone, Abbie nodded. "Yeah, and a couple cops got killed there, too."

"So who's your guy?"

"His name's Carl Polchinski. He's got three addresses, and one of 'em's in Tarrytown."

"Give me the address, I'll pick this cop-killer's ass up right away."

Abbie hesitated. "If you give me a bit, I can—"

"I told you before, Mills, this is *my* case. I'll pick Polchinski up—give me the address."

Reluctantly, Abbie gave it over. "Hell, that's a block from my house. I'll be there in five. Text you when it's done."

Abbie sighed as she ended the call. Maybe she'd be lucky and Polchinski would be in one of the two Sleepy Hollow addresses.

By the time she drove back home from White Plains, the text messages she got from Jones revealed that she wasn't particularly lucky, as Polchinski was nowhere to be found at either his sister's or his girlfriend's.

She then texted Costa to see if she'd had better luck.

Moments after the text, she got a call from Irving's cell phone. "Lieutenant, we've got a problem. I'm at the home of Maryann Polchinski in Tarrytown—there's been an officer-involved shooting. Detective Lisa-Anne Costa just shot a man named Carl Polchinski."

Abbie just stared ahead for several seconds before finally managing to gather up the wherewithal to say, "You have *got* to be kidding me!"

THIRTEEN

SLEEPY HOLLOW, NEW YORK

JANUARY 2014

AS SOON AS Jenny saw the look on her older sister's face, she knew that something really horrible had happened. Abbie was spitting nails and looking like she was about to rip someone's face off.

"What happened?" Jenny was sitting in a corner, working on her laptop while Crane was off in another corner reading through Whitcombe-Sears's *grimoire*. Jenny's own Latin wasn't anywhere near good enough to be of use to Crane's search, so she was poring over the Internet, trying to find something useful about the type of magic that Mercier used on the crosses.

"We finally get a damn lead on this whole thing, someone connected to three of the break-ins. But before we can question him, Costa goes and *shoots* him."

Aghast, Jenny asked, "Why'd she do *that*?"

"I didn't get to ask her, but Irving was on the scene to deal with it. He said it looked like a clean shoot. Costa said Polchinski took a shot at her, and Polchinski did have a recently fired .45 in his hands." Abbie shook her head. "That's also *all* he had on him. No cell phone, nothing else. According to Irving, his mother saw him for the first time in three weeks this morning, and all he had with him when he showed up at her doorstep at five in the morning was the .45. And according to Jones, the girlfriend and the sister also hadn't seen him in three weeks. So we're back to square one thanks to Costa's itchy trigger finger."

Jenny frowned. "This is the same Detective Costa who stepped all over the Cortlandt Museum thing, right?"

Abbie nodded.

"That's a little too convenient."

"What do you mean?"

Jenny stood up from the seat and stretched her back, the vertebrae cracking. She'd been spending *way* too much time sitting. "I mean, we already know the robbery attempt up in Ticonderoga was an inside job. They had a member of the coven working for the museum. So what about down here? Nobody more inside than a cop. And then she conveniently shoots the only lead we have on where this coven is."

The look Abbie was giving Jenny now was like a

knife right in her belly. It was the same expression that Abbie had on her face as a teenager, right after the incident in the woods. Jenny had insisted to the grown-ups—against Abbie's express wishes—that they had seen some kind of monster. The whole time Jenny was pouring her heart out, Abbie gave her the same look she was giving Jenny now. Then, when Abbie was asked if she would corroborate what her sister said, she had said no. Abbie had denied everything.

That started both of them down a couple of very bad roads, roads that remained separate until very recently. Ironically, both of them were rescued by August Corbin, albeit separately. And it took Corbin's death to bring them together.

Abbie then turned away. "I don't like it. She's a *cop*."

"Yeah, well, so was Andy Brooks."

That got Abbie to turn back. Brooks had been a fellow lieutenant under Corbin, who turned out to be a servant of Moloch, the demon they'd spent the last several months battling. Even after his death at Moloch's hands, he'd continued to be an undead servant of Moloch—among other things, he was the one who facilitated Serilda's last attempt at resurrecting herself.

Jenny continued. "Why didn't she wait for you to go into the mother's place?"

"She was home, she said she was a block away."

Putting her hands on her hips, Jenny said, "That's pretty convenient, too."

Abbie closed her eyes and blew out a long breath. "All right, let's check Costa's place out. Dunno how I'm gonna get a warrant, but—"

Unable to believe her ears, Jenny cried, "We don't have *time* for a warrant! There's only a few hours before sunset. We need to get over there *now*, and there isn't time to do it legally."

"Yeah." Abbie shook her head. "I was really enjoying being a cop again, too. Fine, let's get over there, and hope she has her broomstick and cauldron in the living room."

"Eureka!"

Jenny jumped in surprise, and turned to look at Crane, whose presence she had temporarily forgotten. He'd been unusually quiet.

"Please tell me that's a good eureka, Crane," Abbie said.

"It is indeed, Lieutenant." Crane was actually grinning. "I have, at last, located the appropriate spell in this tome."

"Good. What's the next step?"

"Memorizing it." Crane rose and stretched his back. Jenny held back a chuckle as his vertebrae made the exact same snapping sounds that Jenny's had a few moments ago.

"Thought just looking at it got you to memorize it."

"Not quite." Crane took a sip of the mug of tea he had been nursing. "My being eidetic allows me to recall what the words on the page look like at any time. However, there is the rather important matter of pronunciation. That will require rehearsal, preferably in solitude."

Abbie smiled. "Lucky for you, we were just leaving. We'll keep you posted."

THE DRIVE TO Costa's house in Tarrytown was a quick one—Abbie made sure to take a roundabout route that wouldn't take them past the nearby house owned by Polchinski's mother, since that was a crime scene.

Breaking into the place proved to be fairly simple, though it required both of them to do it. Abbie was, to Jenny's annoyance, the better lockpick and got into Costa's back door in thirty seconds, but Jenny was the one who knew the universal stop code for the alarm system that Costa used.

"How'd you know that?" Abbie asked in an accusing tone.

Jenny grinned, recalling the many things she picked up on while hanging out with the Weavers militia group. "I refuse to answer that question without my attorney present, Officer."

"Hardy har har." Abbie shook her head and entered the kitchen. "The good news is, we're pretty unlikely to be interrupted. Officer-involved shooting usually means interviews and paperwork for at least the rest of your shift. Costa won't be coming home for hours yet."

They moved into the living room. Jenny was disappointed to see no broomstick, nor a cauldron, just a lot of beige furniture. "Shouldn't witches be better interior decorators?"

Abbie shrugged. "Maybe it's her way of staying incognito."

Looking around, Jenny spied a police file on the coffee table. She made a beeline for it and started flipping through it.

"Hey!" Abbie practically ran across the room and snatched the file folder out of Jenny's hand. "You're not supposed to look at it."

Jenny stared at Abbie as if she were insane. "Says the woman who just committed a felony to get into this room."

Abbie just stared back, then looked away to read the file.

Smiling, Jenny decided that Abbie's looking away first was a moral victory. Besides, she was just going to read over her shoulder anyhow.

"Oh, man. She was already looking into Polchinski." Abbie sat down on the beige couch and started flipping through pages. "One of her CIs gave Polchinski up. She was in the middle of looking into him when I called her." She flipped another page and then chuckled. "One of the notes says 'no fixed address.' She was probably turning cartwheels when I gave her one."

Now Jenny was confused. "I thought she was the bad guy."

"I don't think so." She flipped another page. "Here are his phone records. Only calls he made in the last three weeks were to one New York City number. Three weeks ago was also when he stopped talking to his family and his girlfriend."

Peering at the phone records, Jenny noted a variety of phone calls prior to mid-December, and then only this one 347 number after that.

There was also a note scrawled on the side that read, "Run this #."

Jenny looked at her sister. "She hadn't checked that number yet?"

"Doesn't look it." Abbie pulled out her cell phone. After a few rings: "Hey, Jones. Listen, I need you to pull a phone record."

After she gave this Jones person the number, Jenny heard a tinny male voice say, "Hang on, I think I know that number. Lemme check." A few seconds later, he said, "Yeah, that's what I thought. It's a burner phone. But I think I know where it's from."

"Where?" Abbie asked sharply.

"Okay, last year some kids had a meth ring going over at the high school. They all used burner phones that they got down in the Bronx. Prob'ly thought they were being clever. But all the phones they used had the same exchange, and it was this one."

Jones then gave an address on West 238th Street in the Bronx.

"Thanks, Jones, I owe you one." She ended the call and then grabbed Jenny's arm. "C'mon, we're taking a drive to the city."

As Jenny allowed her sister to pull her toward the back door, she asked, "Aren't we gonna check the rest of this place?"

Abbie shook her head. "I don't think Costa's our bad guy. I think she's a stone-cold bitch for freezing me out of the investigation, since if we'd cooperated, we'd be closer to finding our coven, but I think she was on the same track as we were. We just gotta follow it."

"What about the judge's order to keep me in Westchester?"

Abbie shrugged. "I won't tell the judge if you won't."

Jenny grinned, pleased at forcing her sister to take another step down the road to the dark side.

It took twenty minutes on the Saw Mill River Parkway to get into the Bronx, the northernmost of the five boroughs of New York City. She got off at the exit for Broadway, which was only the second exit in the Bronx, and then drove down that road to a bodega right on the corner of West 238th Street, underneath the elevated train.

Walking in, Jenny saw a fairly typical bodega

setup: narrow aisles with shelves stuffed floor-to-ceiling with a variety of *stuff*, ranging from candy to staple foods to toiletries to drinks of every type, from milk and juice to sodas from all over the world to various brands of beer.

A Latino man sat behind the bulletproof Plexiglas with a small window through which to exchange merchandise and payment. Behind him, Jenny saw a bunch of disposable cell phones hanging from a rack.

The clerk put down the copy of the *Daily News* he'd been reading. "Can I help you?" he asked in a bored tone.

Holding up her badge with one hand, Abbie pointed at an upper corner of the bodega with the other. "I'm Lieutenant Mills, and I need to know if you still have your security feed from three weeks ago."

Frowning, the clerk said, "You ain't from the 50th. That badge ain't even NYPD. Whatchoo want here, lady?"

"I just told you. I'm from Sleepy Hollow, and I think a person responsible for the death of ten people, including *four cops*, purchased a burner phone here three weeks ago. Two of the cops who were killed *were* NYPD at the museum last night." She pointed at the newspaper, which had the MCNY break-in on the front page. "You can read all about it while I look at your footage."

Holding up both hands, the clerk said, "Hey, it's

cool. I didn't know this was about no cop-killing. Yeah, I got everything from the last year backed up on a flash drive. Gimme five, I'll make a copy for you."

While they waited for the clerk to copy the flash drive, Abbie wandered over to the wire rack that held copies of newspapers. She grabbed another copy of the *News* that had the front-page story on the MCNY break-in. There were formal portraits of the two cops who were killed and a long shot of the museum with Irving and some short, stout lady standing on the big staircase in front of it. Irving looked even more like a stewed prune than usual.

The clerk came back in less than five minutes with a flash drive that was shaped like a duck.

"That's five bucks for the drive and seventy-five cents for the paper," the clerk said as he slid the former through the opening in the Plexiglas.

Abbie just gave the clerk her patented death glare.

Without missing a beat, the man added, "But for you, on the house!"

"Thank you."

"That's all December. Anything else I can help you with?"

"Actually, yeah." She rattled off the number on Polchinski's phone records. "You know when you sold that phone?"

"Normally, I say no, but after those kids used my phones for their filthy drugs, I keep track of *every-*

thing in a spreadsheet, and . . . Hey!" His eyes widened. "That was Sleepy Hollow, too! *Ay, dios,* you people have some kind of crime wave epidemic up there?"

Jenny just laughed, which diluted the effect of Abbie's death glare. "Do you know when you sold this one?"

"Yeah, yeah, hang on a sec." The clerk went over to a battered old laptop that looked like it had a busted hinge. After a few keystrokes and peering at the screen for several seconds, he said, "Here we go. It sold on the tenth at one-oh-seven p.m. Cash."

Shaking her head, Abbie said, "Figures. Can I borrow that laptop?"

Jenny could tell that the clerk was about to say no on general principles, but then he got another look at the death glare, and then unplugged it from its power cord and two USB cords and handed it through the slot in the Plexiglas without a word.

As they found a corner of the bodega to stand with a bit of privacy, Jenny regarded her sister with something like admiration. "He changed his tone pretty quick."

"That guy relies on the local cops in case he ever gets robbed. They find out he got in the way of a cop-killer investigation, he's gonna find himself at the bottom of the local precinct's list. It may be a crime, but people obstruct justice all the time, and mostly we don't care. But you do *not* mess with a cop-killer."

Calling up the files on the flash drive, she found the footage from the tenth of December last year. It was a single video file, and she scrolled ahead to early afternoon.

At one o'clock, she played it at normal speed. Five minutes in, Abbie saw someone enter the bodega that caused her to say, "Oh, crap."

"Who is it?" Jenny did not recognize the woman in question. "Is that Costa?"

Abbie shook her head, but said nothing.

Within two minutes, the woman purchased a burner phone from a different clerk, as well as a bottle of some pineapple-flavored soda and a chocolate bar.

Closing the laptop, Abbie handed it back to the clerk with a quickly muttered thank-you, and then headed out the door.

Jenny ran to catch up with her sister, who was moving at so quick a pace that Jenny, despite her longer legs, was having trouble keeping up.

"Abbie, who *was* that?"

When she got to the car she stared right at Jenny and held up the *News,* pointing at the woman next to Irving. Jenny realized that it was the same woman who was on the footage.

"You were right," Abbie said. "It *was* an inside person. But not Costa. The person who bought Polchinski's burner phone was Irving's old partner, Beth Nugent."

FOURTEEN

BRONX, NEW YORK

OCTOBER 2013

BETH LOOKED AT the other three women in the large, well-appointed living room of her house on Delafield Avenue in Riverdale, an upscale neighborhood of the Bronx. She sat on the large recliner that was perpendicular to the couch, and facing the rocking chair. A coffee table sat between all of them, and Beth had just lit the bayberry candle that sat at the center of it. The autumn sun was setting outside on this early October night.

Formally, she said, "The October 2013 gathering of the Coven of Serilda of Abaddon shall now come to order." Then she leaned back and smiled. "Let's get to it, okay?"

"Get to *what*, exactly?" Frieda asked from her spot on the rocking chair. She moved back and forth, the curved legs of the chair making a divot in the green carpet. "Look at us. We down to *four*. This ain't no coven, it's a damn book club with delusions'a grandeur."

Stacy sat cross-legged on the couch closer to Frieda. "I dunno, felt like a coven when we took care of that delivery guy."

Frieda held up both hands. "I admit, it felt *good* to fry his ass after what he pulled, but we coulda just reported him to the cops, too. The kid was just a college student who got greedy and handsy. I don't mean to be rude or nothin', but we been gettin' together every month 'cause our moms and grand-mothers and great-grandmothers did, and we been studying the texts, and we been doin' the whole sis-terhood thing, and we been *waitin'*. Well, I'm sick'a waitin'. Serilda's been dead for two hundred and fifty years and she's gonna be dead for another two hundred and fifty years."

"Don't be so sure of that," Sophia said in her quiet voice. As always, she kept her head down so that Beth saw more of her blond hair than her face. Her hands were sitting demurely in her lap on the couch. "The signs are all for her returning this month. There were several strange animal deaths, reports of possessions are up, and the blood moon next week is the most powerful one in decades."

"You said that *last* fall, too, Sophia. Every damn blood moon, you—"

"This is different!" Sophia actually looked up at that. Her hands were still placed demurely on her lap, but her voice had risen to almost a conversational tone.

Beth finally decided to speak up. "It isn't just the signs Sophia saw. Death is active in Sleepy Hollow."

Frieda snorted. "Since when do you get all flowery?"

Rolling her eyes, Beth said, "I don't mean the concept or event of death, I mean capital-D Death—the Horseman of the Apocalypse. He's risen from the grave, and he's already killed Reverend Knapp and Sheriff Corbin and some farmer."

Stacy shook her head. "You know I was saying we should've killed that sheriff years ago, right?"

"No." Beth shook her head emphatically. "Delivery boys and other scum-suckers are one thing, but we can't go around killing cops. Trust me, I used—"

"—to be one, we know, we know." Stacy stuck her tongue out at Beth. "We heard it the first fifty times. Anyhow, I guess the Horseman doesn't care about being dainty the way we do."

Frieda folded her arms. "So what's this *mean,* exactly?"

"It means Serilda's allies are finally making a *real* move," Beth said. "Not this pussyfooting around they've been doing. Which means that Sophia's signs are probably *real* ones."

"I'll believe it when I see it." Frieda shook her head.

Sophia actually stood up from the couch, which was the most aggressive move she'd ever made in

Beth's presence, and faced Frieda. "Why do you keep *doing* that? We're trying to do something *important* here, and the rest of us take it seriously! If you're not going to, why don't you just *quit* the way Miriam and Rachael and Kirsten and Gretchen did?"

Beth had never seen Frieda's eyes go as wide as they were now. She had stopped rocking the chair and planted her feet on the carpet. "Easy, girl! I ain't sayin' we should quit, I'm sayin' that we heard this song before. Right now, all we got is a dead sheriff an' a dead priest."

"A dead *immortal* priest," Stacy said. "That's some serious mojo right there."

"Could just be some demon making a power play." Frieda shook her head. "Look, I'd love it if you were right, Sophia, but I just can't get my hopes up again. I'm gettin' too old t'get excited about somethin' that probably ain't gonna happen."

You are a fool to doubt, Frieda Abernathy.

Beth looked up and around her house. The voice seemed to come from everywhere and nowhere, and it felt as if it were echoing off her bones. She shivered, as the temperature in the house suddenly lowered.

Suddenly, Sophia screamed, and then her body tensed, her arms thrust outward. The bayberry candle went out and the lights in the house flickered for a moment.

Jumping to her feet, Beth moved toward Sophia,

but then the smaller woman opened her eyes and stared right at Beth—her eyes had gone completely black. Beth stumbled back for a moment, almost falling back into the recliner before she regained her footing.

"Be assured," came a version of Sophia's not-as-timid-as-usual voice from her mouth, "that Serilda will arise on the night of the blood moon. My minion is already at work. You must all be ready." She walked past the coffee table and into the center of the living room.

"For what?" Stacy asked. "And who are you?"

"It's Moloch," Beth said quickly, annoyed at Stacy for not recognizing one of Serilda's strongest allies amongst demonkind.

Sophia smiled viciously, an expression that didn't really fit on her face. "To answer your question, Stacy O'Connor, you must be ready for victory. Death has arisen, and War will follow soon, then Conquest and Famine. The Witnesses have also been called: they are a man and a woman named Crane and Mills, and their role will be to fall before us to prove our might. The end of days has come, and all who walk with the Horsemen will revel in our dominance."

Stacy grinned. "Sounds good to me."

"Excellent. You will see your mistress soon."

Then Sophia collapsed to the carpeted floor. Beth moved to catch her even as she felt the temperature of the room warm back up.

As Beth guided Sophia back to the couch, Frieda said, "What the *hell*?" She had risen from the rocker and was just standing by the coffee table with a look of annoyance on her face.

"What the hell what?" Stacy said, scooting over on the couch to leave room for Sophia to lie down. "This is what we've been waiting for."

"Oh no it ain't," Frieda said emphatically. "She okay?"

Beth nodded. "Just needs to catch her breath."

In a very weak voice, Sophia said, "That—that was—*very* creepy."

Stacy stood with her hands on her hips. "I thought the idea was to bring Serilda back. We've waited two centuries for this. How is it *not* what we've been waiting for?"

Frieda pointed an accusatory finger at Stacy. "Yeah, we been waitin' for *Serilda*. You see the mistress anywhere in this room? All's I saw was Moloch taking possession of one of our own like nobody's business and *telling* us that *he's* resurrecting Serilda. Who the hell is he to do that? She's *our* mistress, and I for damn sure don't want no demon telling *me* when *he's* resurrecting her."

"That's enough!" Beth cried before Stacy could say anything. "Look, Moloch's a heavy hitter. We can *not* afford to piss him off. If he wants Serilda, that's good for us. Means we finally get our mistress back."

Frieda shook her head. "I guess."

Then Sophia fainted.

"Dammit. Stacy, call 911, we need to get her to a hospital."

Snorting, Frieda said, "Whatcha gonna tell the EMTs? 'Sorry, guys, she fainted after a demon possessed her ass'?"

Glowering at Frieda, Beth said, "We'll tell them she fainted and we don't know why. C'mon, help me put her feet up."

THE NEXT FEW days went very poorly for Beth Nugent.

That meeting was the last time she saw Frieda. She slipped out while the EMTs were taking Sophia to Montefiore Medical Center, and shortly after that Frieda had her phones terminated. All attempts at communication were met with busy signals, disconnection notices, and bounced email messages.

Sophia slipped into a coma, her small, frail body unable to handle the strain of possession by Moloch.

And then, on top of everything else, Serilda's resurrection was stopped by the very two Witnesses that Moloch had informed them of. They were a cop and some British guy, and they managed to find Serilda's bones—Beth had had no idea that they were buried underneath the old armory—and burn them.

After that, they heard nothing from Moloch. Sophie continued to lie in a hospital bed, strange things continued to happen in Sleepy Hollow, and Beth had had enough of it.

"So what do you suggest we do?" Stacy asked at their All Hallows gathering.

"Frieda, wherever she is, was right: we shouldn't be counting on others to bring our mistress back. I've been doing some research." Beth pulled out an old text she'd found through one of her contacts at a library in England. "There are medals that Washington gave out during the Revolutionary War."

"Wait," Stacy said, "the Congressional Crosses?"

Beth blinked. "You know about those?"

Stacy smiled. "Back in 1785, a witch who killed a couple of members of Washington's family, and tried to kill Martha Washington, was an ancestor of mine. The story's been a major one in my family. Those crosses can be used to stop death."

Nodding, Beth said, "Well, you're not the only ancestor who has history with this cross. Sophia listed me as her next of kin and emergency contact, so I got to dig through her apartment. She's got one of these crosses. One of her relatives, a guy named Jebediah Cabot, was awarded one by the Continental Congress, and they kept it in the family ever since. Based on what I read, we can use the crosses to cast a spell that'll resurrect the mistress—but we have to wait for the new year. Once eight half-moons have gone by, we can use six of the crosses to get her back. There are a couple in New York, and I can get my hands on those two no problem. But we need three more, which is why you are about to apply for a job in Ticonderoga."

Stacy frowned. "What the hell's in Ticonderoga? For that matter, *where* the hell is Ticonderoga? Isn't that where they make the pencils?"

"What matters to you is that one of the Congressional Crosses is up there. You need to keep an eye on it and figure out the best way to steal it. We're gonna need it in January to resurrect the mistress." She smiled. "And it's about four or five hours' drive north of here. Nice little town, you'll love it."

"If you say so. What'll you be doing in the meantime?"

Beth sighed. "The two people who stopped Moloch are the Witnesses he mentioned, which mostly means they're gonna be a pain in Moloch's ass."

"Fine by me," Stacy said. "He's a presumptuous asshole. Frieda wasn't my favorite person in the world, but she was right about one thing—that should've been *us* bringing the mistress back, not him."

"Next time it *will* be us, you can count on that for damn sure. And we'll need to be ready for Ichabod Crane and Abigail Mills."

Stacy frowned. "Who names their kid Ichabod?"

Beth shrugged. "Someone in England. He's a professor at Oxford, and Mills is a cop. In fact, get this—she used to be Corbin's partner."

Rolling her eyes, Stacy said, "Gotta love it. She taking his place?"

"No, that's the good part. The guy they put in charge is my old partner from when I was a uniform—Frank Irving."

"Isn't he the one whose daughter is a cripple?"

"Hey," Beth said, pointing a finger at Stacy, "Macey's a good kid."

"Whatever." She took out her smartphone and Googled Ticonderoga.

For her part, Beth also took out her phone. She wanted to check in and see how Sophia was doing.

Just a few more months, and she'd be able to fulfill the coven's long-term mission. And nobody—not these two Witnesses and not her ex-partner—was going to stand in her way.

FIFTEEN

SLEEPY HOLLOW, NEW YORK

JANUARY 2014

ABBIE DROVE THE entire way back to Sleepy Hollow from the Bronx in silence. Before hitting the road, she texted Irving to tell him to be at the armory as soon as possible, and Jenny read the text he sent back when she was on the Saw Mill headed north saying he'd be there in ten minutes.

This meant he was already there waiting, alongside Crane, when they got to the Batcave.

After spending the entire drive up trying to figure out how to explain things to Irving, she was no more sure how to do it than she was when she recognized Beth Nugent's face on the bodega security footage.

She entered to see Irving standing with his arms folded, Crane sipping tea with the *grimoire* from Whitcombe-Sears closed under his elbow.

Procrastinating a bit on talking to Irving, she said to her fellow Witness: "I take it you've got the spell all nice and memorized?"

Crane nodded. "I now merely await a location in which to cast it."

"Well, we're getting closer to that." She let out a long breath and turned to Irving. "We got a break in the case, and you're not gonna like it."

And then she just dove in and told him everything, including the stuff he already knew about Ippolito's deal all the way through to seeing security footage of Nugent buying the same burner phone that Polchinski had been calling for the past three weeks.

Irving was quiet for several seconds. Abbie hadn't known him very long, and still had trouble reading him. She frankly had no idea how the captain would react to this news. Evidence to date suggested a fairly measured reaction—Irving had yet to demonstrate any capacity for flying off the handle—but it was often the quiet ones who exploded without warning.

To her relief, he simply folded his arms. "So let me see if I got this straight. You're accusing my former partner, someone who's been in my home, someone who babysat my kid, of committing mass murder in the name of resurrecting a demon-powered witch, all on the say-so of a guy making a deal to get off on a B-and-E charge?"

Jenny muttered, "I liked the way Abbie put it better."

"Look, Captain, I know it's far-fetched, but we don't have anything else to go on. Besides, we only have her word for what happened at the Met. She knows the security well enough there, and she's in a position to keep them from reporting it. She didn't get seriously hurt at all at MCNY—"

"Neither did I, neither did one of the officers, neither did the museum chief of security," Irving said, "so that doesn't prove a damn thing. And before you mention the burner phone, that's still a real flimsy connection to Polchinski."

"And if we were building a case to present to the DA, I'd agree with you," Abbie said tartly, "but we're not. We're trying to stop the resurrection of a very powerful witch who will likely go on a killing spree."

Crane added quietly, "Your use of future tense is inaccurate, Lieutenant. Serilda has already killed dozens, both in my time and in the present day, and her followers are responsible—"

Irving snapped. "I *know* what her followers are responsible for, Crane!" He shook his head. "I just don't buy that my ex-partner is one of them."

Standing up, Crane moved toward Irving. "I'm aware, Captain, that the bond you forged over your mutual humping of your radio car is a strong one."

Despite the seriousness of the situation, it still took all of Abbie's willpower not to burst out laughing at that. In her peripheral vision, she saw Jenny was also trying to hold in a laugh. There were times when laughing at Crane's malapropisms and attempts at modern slang were the only things that got Abbie through a day.

"However—" Crane tried to continue, but Irving stepped over him.

"No, you're not aware, Crane. You have no idea what my life has been like, and I'll thank you not to presume." Irving's tone had gotten calmer, but no less snippy.

Crane hesitated to respond, but Abbie did not. "Look, Captain, we just followed the evidence—it may be flimsy, but it's all we've got and *we're running out of time.* It'll be sunset soon. We need to find your friend, and we need to find her *now.*"

Shaking his head, Irving paced to a corner of the armory. "I'm not buying it. There's no way she could've kept something like this from me."

That was the straw that broke Abbie's back. "Are you *kidding* me? Look around this room, Captain. All the crap we've got piled in here is a monument to Corbin—my mentor, my *best friend,* my *partner*—keeping an entire part of his life away from me. He'd been hunting demons since before I met him, he even brought my *sister* into it"—she pointed at Jenny, who seemed to cringe—"and I had *no idea* until after he died."

Crane approached Irving and put a hand on his shoulder. "The lieutenant speaks the truth, Captain. Katrina was my wife, yet she also hid a second life from me. We all of us have had things kept from us by those we held dear. And both Sheriff Corbin and my wife engaged in deception with the best of intentions—if Miss Nugent is what we believe she is, then her intentions are far less honorable, and far more dangerous for that."

Jenny spoke up. "I know it sucks. I remember how devastated I was when I was a teenager, and the older sister that I worshipped and would've done anything for threw me under the bus."

Abbie winced. "Jenny—"

She held up a hand. "Don't worry about it, Abbie, I'm not bringing it up to ding you for it, I'm just reminding Captain Happy here that people are more complicated than you think they are. We *all* have stuff to hide, and we all keep things to ourselves. You just told Crane that he doesn't know you—well, maybe you don't entirely know this Nugent chick. Get the hell over it."

"For that matter," Abbie added, "Moloch taunted Crane right before Christmas, said Crane would betray me. No way *that's* gonna happen—except maybe it will. We just don't *know*."

Irving let out a breath through his teeth and then removed his phone from his jacket pocket. "Let me call her, and—"

Reaching out to grab his wrist, Abbie cried out, "No! That's like warning her we're coming. She already thinks she's got one over on us. Let's let her think that."

Now Irving glared down at her. "If you'd give me

a chance, Lieutenant, I was gonna say, 'Let me call her and make her think we're on a different track.' Lull her into a false sense of security."

Abashed, Abbie removed her hand from Irving's wrist. "Sorry."

"I didn't just fall off the turnip truck." He shook his head and started fondling the surface of his smartphone. "I don't like it, but I also know better than to argue with all three of you—especially when you're right." He put the phone to his ear. "Hey, Beth. Listen, we got a line on one of the people involved with the thefts. Yeah, Lieutenant Mills has a CI who pointed her to a second-story guy up in Greenwich. We're heading into Connecticut to check it out. You want in?"

Abbie couldn't make out what Nugent was saying in reply, but she approved of Irving's tactic.

"Okay, well, I'll let you know whether or not it turns into anything. Later."

Crane nodded approvingly. "Well played, Captain."

"Thanks." Irving pocketed the phone. "She said she's visiting a friend in the hospital, which probably had about as much truth in it as what I said. She lives in a house in the North Bronx—been in her family forever. I suggest we get a move on before the moon comes up."

Jenny moved over to the file cabinet. "Let me just get our protection."

Confused, Abbie watched her sister. "Protection?"

"Yeah. When I was going through trying and failing to organize this monstrosity last night—"

Unable to resist, Abbie interrupted. "Let me guess, you got sidetracked?"

"Bite me entirely, sis. *Anyhow,* I found something Corbin dug up a few years back." She started rummaging through one of the file cabinet drawers, and then pulled out a rolled-up scroll. After shutting the drawer, she unrolled the scroll on the table, revealing an ink drawing of a circle with both a pentagram and a naked human figure inside it, the figure's arms and legs overlaying four of the spokes of the pentagram, with the head overlapping the fifth spoke.

Crane stared at it almost reverently. "An Agrippa pentagram. At Oxford, we regularly decried such things as Renaissance superstition. I was forced to revise that opinion when I observed General Washington use one as a protection from one of Serilda's attempts on us." He stared at Jenny. "As I recall, the talisman requires a key word to be spoken to be effective?"

Jenny nodded. "From what Corbin told me, I say the magic word, and anyone touching the scroll is protected from all magic or magical harm for the next twenty-four hours."

"Which is it?"

"Huh?" Jenny asked, sounding confused.

"If it is from magical harm, that is one thing, but from all magic? If so, I must refrain from touching the scroll."

Frowning, Jenny asked, "What? That's crazy. This lady rips people's limbs and heads off."

Abbie, however, had figured it out. "If you're protected from magic, you can't cast the spell."

"Indeed. I shall have to rely upon the three of you to protect me."

Smiling, Abbie said, "That's what we do. Protect each other. Only way to stop the bad guys is if we have each other's backs." That last part she added with an apologetic look at her sister.

For her part, Jenny just looked away. Sentiment hadn't been a strong suit of Jenny's since the incident in the forest, and Abbie had to admit that she only had herself to blame for that. If Abbie hadn't—as Jenny had so eloquently put it a few minutes ago—thrown her younger sister under the bus, she might not have turned into the surly adult standing before her now.

"All right, then, let's armor up," Jenny said, putting a hand on the scroll.

Abbie did likewise.

Irving hesitated. "Sorry, just trying to wrap my brain around all this. Again."

"I sympathize, Captain," Crane said quietly, "but we must hurry."

"I'm fine," Irving said as he put his hand on a corner of the scroll. "Any time I have trouble with all this nonsense, I remember Paul Short."

Wincing, Abbie nodded in understanding. Short was a lab tech, and an old friend of Irving. Abbie had met him once or twice on cases. He was shot to ribbons by the Horseman Death, while Irving watched—and almost got killed himself. That was the event that finally brought Irving over into the light side, as it were. Up until then he'd been supportive, but not entirely believing. But seeing a decapitated man blow away an old friend of his with a Colt M4A1 had a way of forcing the captain's belief in the things that went bump in the night.

Jenny looked around at the two of them. "Ready?"

Abbie nodded. Irving said, "Not in the least, but go ahead, anyhow."

After nodding back, Jenny closed her eyes, took a breath, and then said, *"Da nobis auxilium de magicis."*

A flash of light blinded Abbie temporarily, and she had to blink the spots out of her eyes.

When her vision cleared, the scroll was gone, and she could smell the residue of smoke in the air, like a match that had just been blown out.

"I don't suppose Corbin had any more of those?" Abbie asked as she continued to blink away spots that danced in her vision from the flash of light as the scroll burned.

"If he did, he didn't tell me," Jenny said.

Crane raised an eyebrow. "As I believe we all may attest, his lack of speech on the subject is not indicative of anything—and is also of little moment right now. I suggest we proceed with all due haste to Bronck's land."

They filed quickly out of the armory, Abbie

pausing to turn out the lights and lock the door. Crane was polite enough to wait for her to finish that, and as she turned the key, she asked, "So what was that phrase that Jenny used?"

"Simply translated," Crane replied, "it means 'give us protection from magic.' It is almost poetic in its concision."

"Concise is nice. So's poetic." She turned to stare up at Crane. "I just wish we had more of them. Or we could make it last longer than a day. Or we could use it on you and still let the spell be cast." She let out a sigh. "But hey, if wishes were horses, we'd be hip-deep in crap."

Crane made one of his faces. "How quaint." Then he cocked his head. "Though, admittedly, it is actually rather a logical progression, since horses are indeed known for producing prodigious amounts of dung." He shook his head. "In any event, if wishes did come true, I doubt you and I would ever have met. I would have survived the war with Katrina and our son, and we would have lived peaceful lives in these United States, perhaps with more children."

Abbie almost made a comment about how she would be in D.C. right now with the FBI, but she couldn't bring herself to voice it. Crane had spoken in a remarkably matter-of-fact tone, but it wasn't quite enough to hide the anguish behind his wistful words of what could've been—what, in her opinion, *should* have been.

But she couldn't bring herself to say *that* out loud, either, as it would sound horribly patronizing.

So she settled for putting a hand on his arm and giving it a friendly squeeze, while looking up at him and smiling warmly.

Crane looked down and provided a similar smile back. "Alas," he said very quietly.

Within a minute, they were outside, where Irving was standing by one of the department's SUVs. The sun was starting to set, painting the western sky over the Hudson River with a magnificent burst of oranges and purples, and casting the Tappan Zee Bridge in a warm glow.

But she couldn't really pause to enjoy the magnificent sunset. She promised herself that she would force herself to do so one of these days. After all, she and Crane were trying to save the world. It wouldn't do to go to all that trouble and not remember what about the world was worth saving.

Irving was holding a set of keys in his hand. "We're getting into rush hour, and the moon'll be up soon. I want a company car that has sirens and lights we can run in case we hit traffic."

Jenny gave the captain a teasing look. "What's this? Abusing police privilege? Captain Irving, I'm *impressed*."

The look fell when Irving whirled on her and pointed a finger. "Don't—not tonight."

Holding up both hands, Jenny said, "Sorry."

Irving got into the driver's seat. Jenny immediately went into the back on the driver's side, and Abbie decided to take shotgun. Crane climbed into the seat behind her.

As Irving started the ignition, Abbie looked over at him. "Look, I'm sorry for what I said. I know this isn't easy for you."

"None of this is easy for any of us. Doesn't mean we don't do it. Like your sister said, I need to get over it."

He put the car into drive and headed out onto Beekman Avenue toward Broadway.

SIXTEEN

New York, New York

JANUARY 2014

BETH NUGENT NEARLY stumbled when she entered Sophia's room at the hospital and found Frieda sitting next to her.

Frieda said, "Hey, Beth" as if she hadn't disappeared for three months. She was looking at Sophia's still-comatose form in the hospital bed. Sophia was a scion of the very wealthy Cabot family, and so her health coverage pretty much boiled down to money-is-no-object. So she got a private room in Mount Sinai Hospital, and had been looked at by many of the best specialists in the world.

Not that any of them had been able to do anything about her condition.

Sophia had also been Beth's ace in the hole. She'd wanted to avoid going after the Whitcombe-Sears Library at first, as that was right under the

Witnesses' noses in Sleepy Hollow, but once Stacy got herself killed without getting the cross in Ticonderoga, she had no choice.

The good news was that she wouldn't need to use Sophia's blood, as a descendant of someone awarded a cross, to enhance the spell. Since she had to kill Whitcombe-Sears anyhow, it was easy enough to get his blood.

Now, though, she was more concerned about her prodigal coven-mate. Putting her hands on her hips, Beth said, "Who the *hell* let you in here?"

"It's a hospital, Beth." Frieda chuckled, but it sounded odd. So did her voice; it was more whispery than usual. "People come in and out all the time."

Beth intended to have some serious words with hospital security after this, but didn't pursue the matter further with Frieda, instead asking, "Fine, then where the hell've you *been*?"

Finally, Frieda turned around and stood up. Beth gasped. The entire left side of her face was scarred and disfigured from what appeared to Beth's ex-cop eyes as multiple stab wounds.

In a much quieter tone, Beth asked, "What happened?"

"Can answer both those questions in one shot. Two nights after Moloch showed up at your house, he showed up at mine. I was all packed and done, gettin' away from all this. I was in this for empowerment, not the apocalypse. I wanted a better world, not a blown-up one." She shook her head. "Guess he was in a bad mood 'cause he couldn't resurrect Serilda. Decided to take it out on my face. Oh yeah, he told me *all* about how those Witnesses he was talkin' about stopped the resurrection an' burned her bones, an' that it was *my* fault for bein' disloyal." She snorted. "I was *never* disloyal to Serilda, not *once*. Anyhow, I been in a hospital bed, too, past few months, recoverin' from this."

Beth moved toward Frieda. "I'm sorry, I had no idea."

"Yeah, well, I wasn't really much in the mood for company. And I didn't want you to have no idea, y'know? I was done with all this nonsense. I only came here to see how Sophia's doin'. But after this? I'm done. Serilda ain't comin' back. Not now."

"Yes, she is," Beth said emphatically. "And it's happening tonight."

"Say what?" Frieda gave her a look of disbelief that was the first sign of the old Frieda that Beth had seen today.

And so Beth explained about the eight half-moons and the Congressional Crosses—one of which was Sophia's and the other five of which she had gathered—and the ritual she was performing tonight.

"I shoulda known." Frieda was looking at Beth with an almost pitying expression. "I read about the museum downtown, and those two places up in

Westchester. That much carnage, figured it had to be you or Stacy."

"Stacy's dead." Beth saw no reason to beat around the bush. "She tried to get one of the crosses up in Ticonderoga, but the two Witnesses stopped her and killed her. Same ones who stopped the mistress from being resurrected in October."

"Wait, Stacy's *dead*?"

Beth nodded.

Frieda shuddered. "Dammit, this is crazy. And honestly, I thought it *was* Stacy who did those killings 'cause some cops were killed. Whatever happened to 'we can't kill cops'?"

"That was before." The words sounded lame even to Beth. "For regular stuff, yeah, you bet, we did *not* want to get on the radar, but this? This is to *resurrect the mistress*. It's the damn brass ring! That's worth paying any price. Look, Frieda, I'm doing this tonight." She reached out and—not knowing how far down the injuries went under her clothes— was sure to grab Frieda's right arm. "I could use your help."

"No." Frieda backed away from Beth's touch. "I told you, I'm done with this. After that crap in October—"

"Don't you understand, what I'm doing tonight is *because* of what happened in October!" Beth blew out a sigh. "Look, you were right that night. We shouldn't have let Moloch get involved. Well, he *isn't* involved in what I'm—what *we're*—doing to-night. Think about it, Frieda—we'll finally have Serilda back. Our mistress can lead us—"

"'Us'?" Now Frieda was laughing at her. "There ain't no 'us' left, Beth! Half our coven walked out on us over the last year, Sophia's in a coma, and Stacy's dead."

Beth couldn't believe that Frieda wasn't under-standing the enormity of what she was about to ac-complish. "The mistress'll be able to wake Sophia up. And with her here, Miriam and the others will come back!"

"You hope."

Shrugging, Beth said, "If not, we'll get new members. Be a lot easier to recruit with Serilda of Abaddon leading the meetings instead of me." She stared Frieda right in the eyes—though the left eye was half covered with scarred flesh. "I'm doing this with or without you, Frieda, but I'd rather do it with you."

She put out a hand.

"You with me, or not?"

For several seconds, Frieda stared at Beth's hand, as if she'd never even seen such a thing before. The low beeps of the monitors connected to Sophia's co-matose form echoed in the suddenly quiet room.

"One condition," Frieda said, still not accepting Beth's hand. "First thing we ask Serilda for is to take care'a Moloch."

That got a laugh out of Beth, as that was the second thing she intended to ask the mistress for, after helping Sophia.

She was, however, concerned that Frieda had not once referred to Serilda as "the mistress," as had been common in the coven for all of Beth's life.

However, she'd worry about that after the mistress was resurrected. "Deal."

Then Frieda put her hand in Beth's. "All right, I'm in. But I'm warning you, I'm *hella* rusty. Ain't cast a spell in months."

"You'll be fine. It's like riding a bicycle."

Beth briefly paid her respects to Sophia, then took Frieda with her to catch the express bus back up to Riverdale. They got off at her stop and walked the rest of the way to the house she'd grown up in, the house that had been in her family for several generations.

As soon as they went inside, Frieda let out a whistle. She was looking down at the living room floor, which was now all hardwood. "Damn, girl. You tore up the carpet?"

In the center of the living room, she had drawn a sigil on the floor, after moving the couch, recliner, rocking chair, and television against the wall and putting the coffee table in the basement. "Had to, you can't draw with chalk on a wall-to-wall."

"I ain't complainin'. If I'd known you had such a nice floor under the rug, I'd'a told you to rip it up years ago."

Beth went through the living room to the dining

room, where she had a safe hidden behind a large photograph that had been taken of her when she was five years old. She sat on her mother's lap, while her grandmother stood behind her mother. On the wall behind them in the photograph was a picture of Beth's great-grandmother, who had died the year Beth was born.

After taking the photo down off the wall, she opened the safe and removed the six Congressional Crosses, as well as the blade she'd stabbed Al Whitcombe-Sears with.

All her planning, all her hard work, it was finally paying off. Now that Frieda was back with her, she knew that victory would be hers—and the mistress's.

SEVENTEEN

BRONX, NEW YORK

JANUARY 2014

ACCORDING TO WHAT Irving told them on the drive down here, Nugent's house had a front door, which she almost never used; a side door off the driveway, which led to a tiny foyer that led to both the kitchen and the living room, which she used fairly often; and a basement door that was down a narrow stone staircase behind the house. Abbie took the seldom-used front door for herself, with Jenny taking the basement and Irving the side door. Abbie chose that configuration on the theory that the side door was likely to be unlocked. Better for Abbie and her sister to use the doors with locks they could pick.

To Abbie's lack of surprise, Irving's only response to her rationale had been "I'll just pretend I didn't hear that part."

Crane remained behind at the SUV, which was

parked one house down the road on Delafield Avenue.

The front door in question was made of wood, with a half-oval etched-glass window just above Abbie's own eye level. Standing on her tiptoes, she saw Nugent placing small pieces of metal—probably the six crosses she'd gathered—on different places on the floor. The etched glass warped the view enough that she couldn't be sure, but it seemed reasonable.

It also meant, as they'd feared, that she'd already had an Independence Cross of her own, and only needed to steal five. Either that, or she'd stolen another one that they managed to miss, but given the body counts at all but one of the sites, Abbie considered that unlikely. And that one exception was the Met, where Nugent had an in. None of the other museums or libraries across the country represented by IYS had an Independence Cross; Abbie had checked that back at the beginning of this process. At the time it was just due diligence, but she was really glad for her police training, which had her check into Nugent and her company as a matter of course.

Something else she had Corbin to thank for.

Which sometimes made up for his keeping all the demon stuff from her. At times, she wondered how much easier dealing with all this nonsense would've been if Corbin had just come out and *told* her. . . .

To Abbie's surprise, the door was unlocked when she tried it. Riverdale was a generally safe neighborhood, but still, leaving a door unlocked seemed imprudent.

Then again, Nugent had the ability to slice people into five pieces. Not much to fear from a burglar there.

Unholstering her Glock, Abbie very carefully did *not* cock it, but held it in a ready position as she opened the door.

As she entered the living room, Nugent turned and gestured at her.

Abbie flinched and held her breath, but then nothing happened.

Nugent was actually smiling. On the cover of the *News* and in the file she'd read previously, the short, broad-shouldered woman looked completely professional and straight. Now, as she was smiling and gesturing at Abbie, she looked completely unprofessional—and damned scary.

"Gotta say, I'm impressed, Lieutenant." Then she whirled and turned toward the doorway to the foyer, where Irving was also standing with his Glock. Nothing happened there, either. "Nicely done, partner. I didn't think you had it in you. Never thought that Frank 'I turned my back on God after Macey's accident' Irving would go for something like an Agrippa talisman."

Abbie blew out a breath through her teeth. If Nugent could tell what they'd done just by how they resisted her magic, then they were dealing with some serious mojo. Not that they didn't think that anyhow, given what she did to all those bodies, but still . . .

"Oh, by the way? The talisman affects you, but not your weapons."

Suddenly, the stock of her pistol grew too hot to touch. Quickly, Abbie dropped it to the hardwood floor. Irving did the same with his a second later.

"I'd watch out if I were you," Nugent added with a chuckle.

"No need," Abbie said. "We already went through that episode of *Mythbusters* up in Ticonderoga. Neither of us had one in the chamber, case you pulled that."

Abbie then heard a clicking sound, prompting Nugent to whirl around and throw out an arm toward the back of the room. The air shimmered like the sky in the desert for just a second, just as Abbie heard the report of a bullet being fired.

Just like at the fort, though, the bullet that Jenny fired from the back door was liquefied.

And then Jenny appeared in the doorway and had to drop her 9 mm as well.

"You guys are good," Nugent said. "I'm impressed. But the thing about old Agrippa? He was big on stopping *black* magic. His little talisman'll keep me from slicing you all to ribbons. But there's other magic that'll still work just fine. *Now*, Frieda!"

Abbie was wondering who the hell Frieda was, when suddenly the house started to melt away. "What is—"

. . .

"—THE PROBLEM HERE, Brian?"

Special Agent Abbie Mills stood and stared at the assistant special agent in charge of her division, Brian Wilhoite, while standing in the doorway to the latter's cramped office in the J. Edgar Hoover Building in Washington.

"No problem, Abbie, we just want Smith to take the lead."

Abbie put her head in her hands. "This is *my* case. I'm the one who figured out that the murders were linked, I should be the one—"

Wilhoite shook his head. "Abbie, stop. Look, you've only been with the bureau for five minutes. This is a serial case, and thanks to the latest victim being the husband of a woman running for Congress, it's a press case *and* a politically sensitive case."

"This is crap, Brian. You think I didn't handle politically sensitive cases in Westchester?"

Grinning, Wilhoite said, "Honestly? No, I don't. Not like this. C'mon, Abbie, you said it yourself: you worked in *Westchester*. I mean, c'mon, what was the most politically charged case you handled up there? When an alderman got his cat stuck in a tree?"

Abbie sighed, wishing she didn't have a Chicago native for an ASAC. "No, because we don't have aldermen in New York."

"Very funny. Look, this is bureau policy. You don't get to take the lead on a case while there's still water behind your ears, you get me?"

"Fine." Abbie turned and left the office, working her way through the cubicles until she reached her own.

Three pink pieces of paper were on her desk, two from Smith saying to call him, one from August Corbin.

Having absolutely no desire to talk to the person to whom Wilhoite had just handed *her* case, she instead chose to return Corbin's message. She hadn't heard from her ex-partner in months.

"Hey, kiddo," he said after answering on the first ring.

"What's up, August?"

"What, a guy can't call his ex-partner to say hi? I mean, you do still *remember* your ex-partner, right? Not forgetting the little people back in the Hudson Valley after you graduated top of your class at Quantico?"

Abbie shook her head. "I think that's a new record."

"What is?" Corbin sounded confused.

"This time you got in the reference to my graduating at the top of my class in under ten seconds."

Corbin laughed. "Can I help it if I'm proud of my protégée?"

"I guess you can't."

"So how're things in FBI Land? Or can't you talk about it with us bumpkin sheriffs?"

"Oh, stop that. Most of the guys here, they wouldn't last five minutes under you." She sighed. "Anyhow, I got a case—a possible serial, one I saw the pattern on and brought to the ASAC. But they gave it to another agent. I get to assist, but—"

"But you're too new. You don't get to be in charge of your own serial killer case first time out of the gate."

"Yeah." Abbie chuckled ruefully. "How do you do that?"

"Do what?"

"Make everything sound reasonable. You said the same thing Wilhoite did, but it made sense coming from you."

"Just my natural charm and good looks."

Abbie rolled her eyes. "We're talking on the phone. And you don't look *that* good."

Corbin chuckled. "Look, kiddo, I'm not one to give advice—"

"Since when?" Abbie asked with a grin.

Ignoring her, Corbin went on. "—but rules like the one that's keeping you off this case were made for ordinary people. It's so people don't get thrown in out of their depth the first time out. And ninety-nine times out of a hundred, the rule's absolutely right. But what you gotta remember is that you're not ordinary. You never have been. You were an extraordinary cop, and you'll be an extraordinary agent. A special special agent."

She could practically hear his grin on that last joke. "Thanks," she said quietly. "I mean it."

"I know you do. Now go catch yourself a serial killer that some other agent'll get all the credit for. Just don't forget that there's an old man in Sleepy Hollow who knows that you're the best."

Abbie was about to reply, when suddenly—

—*she's on a call with Corbin to the Fox Hill Stables just outside town. She moves around to the back of the stables, with Corbin taking the front. She notices Ogelvie's pickup truck, the driver's-side door wide open, which is very much not like him.*

"Mr. Ogelvie? It's Lieutenant Mills."

There's no answer.

She goes inside, and almost trips on a shotgun. Keying her radio, she tells Corbin, "We got a weapon on the ground."

Seconds later, she finds a body. A body without a head. She realizes that it's Jimmy Ogelvie, and he's been decapitated.

As she comes into sight of Ogelvie's barn's double doors, she sees an axe head slam through the wood, splintering it. She hears the sickening squelch of blood, and the awful thud of a body falling to the ground. Fearing the worst, she runs to the barn only to find her second decapitated body in as many minutes—and also the second of her entire life.

It's Corbin.

"*Officer down! Oh, God, officer down!*" *she cries—*

—and then she was back in her dinky cubicle.

"You're dead," she whispered into the phone.

"Excuse me?" Corbin asked.

She stood up, clutching the receiver to her ear. "This isn't right. You're dead, you were killed back in Sleepy Hollow. I never went to Quantico."

"Kiddo, what're you—"

Abbie slammed the phone down and then cried out, "I'm not buying this, Nugent!"

And then she screamed in agony. . . .

FRANK IRVING CAME home from his shift as commander of the 24th Precinct in Manhattan. The promotion had, he felt, been earned. The two-four wasn't the toughest precinct in the city these days—the gentrification of Morningside Heights had reduced the crime rate considerably—but it was still enough of a neighborhood in transition that there was plenty to keep the cops under his command busy.

As soon as he opened the door, Macey came running into his arms at full speed, the impact of her running hug nearly toppling him over. "Welcome home, Daddy."

"Oof." Irving grinned. "Maybe don't build up such a head of steam next time, okay, Little Bean?"

"*Yes,* Dad."

Cynthia was taking her earrings off and had slid out of her heels, but otherwise was still in her suit.

"I just got home myself." She reached for the sideboard and held up several takeout menus, which she fanned out like a poker hand. "What do you want for dinner: pizza, Chinese, Indian, or Thai?"

Irving grinned. "Well, we had pizza last night and I had Chinese for lunch, so I'm for Indian or Thai."

"Well, I had Thai for lunch, so Indian it is."

Macey made a face. "Aw, Mom, last time we got takeout from the Indian place I spent *all night* in the bathroom."

That surprised Irving. "You did? Why's this the first time I'm hearing about it?"

Rolling her eyes, Cynthia said, "Because you could sleep through an earthquake, Frank. I'm fine with doing Thai again for dinner."

"Yay!" Macey now ran to her room.

Irving watched her run, not sure why, but knowing that that was the most amazing sight in the world.

It was also completely wrong.

He lifted his left hand to his face, only to feel the weight of his wedding ring on his finger. It felt heavy, ungainly, as if he weren't used to it.

And he wasn't. This was wrong. Cynthia and he were divorced, and Macey—

—lies broken in the emergency room, doctors and nurses all around her, operating feverishly. Irving's badge allows him into the hallway outside instead of the waiting room, but that proves to be a curse rather than

a blessing. He can see them cutting Macey open, hoping to heal the wounds, to fix the damage, to save her life.

Unable to take it anymore, he goes into the waiting room, where Cynthia is sitting on the couch, tears streaking down her cheeks. "Is she okay? Frank? Frank—"

"—are you okay?"

"No," he said honestly to the woman who may or may not have been his wife. "Something's wrong. With all this. I shouldn't be here."

Cynthia laughed. "What're you talking about, Frank? This is our home. Has been for ages."

"Not mine. Not anymore." He ripped the wedding ring off and tossed it to the floor, then grabbed Cynthia's head, cupping her cheeks in his hands. He could smell her perfume, feel her warmth, yet he knew it couldn't be her. "I wish this was real, Cynthia, but it isn't. Macey can't walk anymore and we aren't married anymore, and this just isn't *real*."

And then he screamed in agony. . . .

"OKAY, THAT'S IT for today. Don't forget, I need your thesis statements in my email box no later than five p.m. on Friday. Any later than that, and it affects your grade. And remember, I have a zero-tolerance policy when it comes to excuses. Doctor's notes won't cover it—pretty much every hospital these days has Wi-Fi."

The students around the room chuckled at Professor Joseph Bieo's words as they got up from their desks, the sound of the chairs scraping on the tile cutting through the laughter that echoed through the lecture hall. Sitting on the side of the room, Bieo's teaching assistant, Jenny Mills, just shook her head.

After the room cleared, Bieo looked at Jenny. "You know what the sad part is? About a quarter of the students will *still* hand in the thesis late. It's human nature. And then I'll give them a B or a C, and then they'll complain about the low grade, having completely forgotten what I said today. Or worse, thinking that what I said didn't apply to *them*."

Jenny smiled at her mentor. "You're a cynical bastard, aren't you?"

Bieo shrugged. "Sadly, it comes with the territory. But enough about these slugabeds. Come Friday, you get to read all their theses and tell me if any of them are worthy. Personally, I don't believe we shall have more than five good ones."

Shaking her head, Jenny said, "I think you're not giving them enough credit. I'm thinking ten."

That got a grin out of Bieo. "Do you wish to put your money where your foot is?"

"Sure." Jenny chuckled. "Ten bucks says I'm closer to right than you are."

"Very well. Up to seven good ones, I win. Eight or more good ones, and you win. But let's make it interesting, shall we? Money is so—so tawdry."

Jenny shook her head again. "First of all, people who try to change a bet from money to something else are people who aren't confident that they're going to win. Second, you just wanted an excuse to use the word *tawdry* in a sentence so you could impress me with your vocabulary."

Bieo bowed. "Guilty as charged. I was going to suggest the loser buy the winner dinner at a restaurant of the latter's choice."

"Which isn't at all fair, because you like gourmet restaurants. I'm a PhD candidate, which means I'm *broke*. Let's stick with ten bucks."

"You're on." Bieo grinned. "Now then, I've got the seminar to teach. Can you meet with Mr. Alvarez at two? Apparently he is having some sort of issue."

Jenny winced. "Okay, I guess? But I've got a session with Mira at two thirty, so Jorge really can't be late like he usually is."

Bieo shook his head. "I forgot that you're mentoring the good Ms. Johnson. Remind me why again?"

Now Jenny rolled her eyes. Bieo was a good professor, a fantastic archeologist, an understanding mentor, but details of everyday life tended to slip by him—which was why he needed a TA in the first place. "Mira's a scholarship student, came up through the foster-care system."

"So?"

Yup, details just flew on by. "My sister and I were raised in foster care. It sucks, it drains the life out of you, and Mira didn't let it get her down."

Shrugging, Bieo said, "You didn't let it get you down, either. And isn't your sister a police officer or some such? Doesn't seem to me as if it's all that much of a detriment if the three of you managed. Either way, I'm sure Mr. Alvarez will, in fact, be late, but I also can't imagine his complaint is of any real moment." He closed his briefcase and moved toward the door. "I will see you at Dr. Hastings's reception this evening."

"Yeah, fine," Jenny muttered. He couldn't remember why she was mentoring Mira Johnson, but he had to remember the stupid reception? She was really hoping his ditziness would get her out of that.

She also had no nice clothes to wear for the reception. The one nice outfit she had was still sitting in a pile on the floor of her bedroom waiting for her to have the money to have it dry-cleaned.

As she packed up her books and laptop she realized she was going to have to call Abbie. It would be a tight fit—Jenny was a bit taller than her younger sister—but she could probably squeeze into one of her suits.

She was looking forward to her session with Mira, who was a good kid. Jorge Alvarez, not so much. Jenny knew that Bieo had fobbed him off on her because the kid was a chronic excuse-maker, Bieo's least favorite thing in the world. And Jorge was probably going to complain the whole time about how unreasonable Bieo was.

Jenny really enjoyed being Bieo's TA. He was eloquent and tall and smart and engaging. It was like studying under an African prince. And she enjoyed just listening to him talk. It was just like listening to Crane. . . .

She blinked. Who the hell was Crane?

And then she remembered, a tall man in a ratty old coat—

—*standing in the doorway to Room 49 of Tarry-town Psychiatric, her home away from home. She hates it here, yet she keeps coming back, because she knows that the world outside isn't safe. It isn't safe for her, and it isn't safe* from *her.*

"Thank you for seeing me, Miss Mills," he says, sounding for all the world like he stepped out of an episode of Downton Abbey.

"Curiosity got the best of me," she replies. Any change in the routine was something worth grabbing at, and some tall British guy dressed like he'd just walked in from a historical reenactment was definitely worth a look. "Plus, I was bored. Who are you? Abbie's new boyfriend?"

"We are amicable. And yes, I am male, but I suspect you are implying something else."

Deciding she likes this one a lot better than the last boyfriend of Abbie's she met—which was years ago, and not even her most recent beau—she asks, "What's your name, Tall, Dark, and British?"

"Ichabod Crane."

Oh, this is too perfect. It really was like she walked into PBS. "What do your friends call you? Icky?"

"Not if they want to remain my friends."

Impressed, she says, "Sense of humor, too."

Then he drops the bombshell. "I've seen the demon in the woods—the one you and your sister saw as children."

Jenny is taken aback by that. This is ridiculous, some guy coming out of nowhere and telling her that he be-lieves her, which is absurd, because nobody believes her ever, not even Abbie, who was there, and—

—that didn't happen! "It's not real!"

Several people turned to look at her funny as she walked through the quad.

Shaking her head, Jenny started walking more quickly toward the archeology department's offices.

"I'm not crazy," she muttered to herself. That whole world was nonsense, with her sister betraying her and British guys from the Revolutionary War and demons possessing her and Corbin helping her and the Weavers and Adams and the training and all the rest of it, and it wasn't real, it couldn't be real, because she was happy here and now, on her way to a PhD, not that crazy woman who spent her ado-lescence and her twenties in and out of loony bins. That wasn't her. *This* was her.

But it wasn't real.

And then she screamed. . . .

THE PART CRANE was least looking forward to was the bloodletting.

He stood next to the police automobile they had arrived in, holding the Congressional Cross he'd been awarded in one hand, a small dagger in the other. At the moment, he was simply waiting for a sign. They weren't even sure that Miss Nugent would be in this house performing the ritual, and it wouldn't do for Crane to waste time casting a counterspell against magics that were being cast somewhere else entirely.

But once he saw a sign that his very nascent spellcasting ability would be required, he would need to slice open his flesh in order to baptize the cross with his own blood. Crane understood better than most the power of blood. The mingling of his blood with that of Death led to his fate and that of the Horseman being intertwined. The revelation that Death was his old friend Abraham van Brunt made that intertwining even more tragic, for he and van Brunt were already all but blood brothers, before Crane's and Katrina's love for each other came between them.

Then there was the golem that Katrina had made for their son, Jeremy, which had grown into a fierce, vicious protector of the boy. Crane could only kill him with the blood of the boy who created him—but Crane's blood, being that of his father, did the trick as well.

And now this. This medal was awarded to him, and as Whitcombe-Sears had said, his own blood would infuse it with great power. Miss Nugent was doing the same with Whitcombe-Sears's own blood, but it was diluted with the passing on of the generations. For once, Crane's being out of his own time was a significant advantage.

Out of the corner of his eye, he caught a flash of light. Turning, he saw that the windows in the dwelling belonging to Miss Nugent were flickering with a light that Crane recognized as being eldritch. That illumination came neither from any candle nor from the lighting bulbs that people in this era used.

The spell was being cast.

And so he took the dagger in his right hand and sliced open his left palm, wincing at the feel of the cold metal on his warm hand, followed by the slickness of the blood that pooled in the cut. Picking up the medal with his right hand, he held his left hand over it, the blood dripping onto the silver.

He started to recite the words he had rehearsed several times in the armory, but then was distracted—

—BY THE SMALL children running about the dock of New York Harbour. One urchin crashed into Crane's leg, and he stumbled back for a bit.

Luckily, Jeremy was by his side and able to stabilize him. "Are you all right, Father?"

Crane brushed a silver hair out of his eyes and looked over at his son, who was a man now, as tall as his father. "I'm well, Jeremy, thank you."

The boy who had collided with his leg had already lost himself in the crowd gathered waiting for the sailing ship that had arrived this morning from England and was in the process of being secured to the dock so that its passengers could disembark.

"It's so—so disorderly here, Father," Jeremy said in a disapproving tone.

Crane smiled. "Perhaps, but that is the nature of a port."

"I'm glad we don't live here in town. And even gladder to be going to Oxford!"

Now Crane's smile dimmed somewhat. But still, he could not deny his son this opportunity.

The last seventeen years had been kind to him and his family. With the colonists' victory in 1783 came an affirmation of the independence they had declared seven years previous to that. In 1788, General Washington was elected to the office of the presidency of the newly United States, and he won reelection in 1792.

It was the 1796 election that truly showed the world that a new age was upon them. President Washington chose not to run for a third term and his vice president, John Adams, was elected. On the fourth of March in 1797, Washington did something that rocked the world to its foundations: he willingly turned over the reins of power to another. Changes in power were supposed to happen via illness, death, or violent change, yet here was Adams bloodlessly seizing power from Washington.

Now, at the turn of the new century, Crane had received a letter from his father.

In truth, he didn't receive it as such. Father had

disowned Crane when he switched sides and took up the cause of the colonists against King George twenty-five years ago, and the last letter he'd received from his father was the one declaring that very fact.

The letter that had arrived at the Crane residence three months ago, however, was addressed to Jeremy and assured him that his rightful place at Oxford University was secured, should he wish to pursue it, as was his legacy.

Apparently, Father's disdain only lasted a generation. Crane would have preferred to have a father who understood why his son made the choices he did, but alas, it was not to be. At the very least, he did not pass on his hatred to Jeremy, or his two daughters, who were innocent of the disagreement between their father and grandfather.

In due course, the sailing ship was secured, and its passengers filed off the vessel one by one. Father was, perhaps not surprisingly, one of the last to do so, as he was walking very slowly and with a cane.

However, he limped his way down the gangplank and walked up to Jeremy, not even giving his son a first glance, much less a second one.

"You must be Jeremy."

"Indeed I am, sir." Jeremy reached out his hand. "It is a great pleasure to finally meet you, Grandfather. I'm eager to begin my studies."

Returning the handshake, Father said, "I'm glad to hear that. I believe that you will enjoy England. It is a *civilized* nation."

Several tart responses ran through Crane's head, and he cast all of them out. He did not wish his first conversation with his father in more than twenty-five years to be an argument.

Instead, he went with a platitude. "You look well, Father."

"I look nothing of the sort," Father snapped. "The voyage here was miserable, exacerbating my already poor health. However, I thought it important to risk the journey in any event, as the Crane legacy *must* live on."

"Ichabod!"

Crane was spared having to find a polite way to respond to his father's comment by the sound of his wife. She was coming through the crowd, their two daughters on either side of her, holding a hand.

When she joined the trio, she smiled. "You must be my father-in-law. I am Katrina Crane." She bowed her head, the bonnet covering her hair that, like Ichabod's, was mostly gray these days. "And these are your granddaughters."

Both girls stepped forward and curtsied properly. "Hello, Grandfather," the oldest said, and the youngest followed with a muttered "Hello."

For the first time, Father's face brightened from the sour expression he'd had from the moment he came out onto the deck of the boat. "You're both very polite little girls. I imagine that comes from the good teachings of your mother."

Crane winced.

"Actually," Katrina said with a mischievous smile, "any politeness you detect from our offspring comes entirely from Ichabod. You will find, sir, that I am a most intemperate woman."

"I doubt that very much." Father's words were solicitous of Katrina, but Crane inferred the insult.

"Father, I *do* wish—"

"You wish *what*, exactly, Ichabod?" Father snapped, turning at last to look at his son. "You committed treason, against the king, against our country, against *me*. And for this treason you have been amply rewarded. The side you chose was victorious. You have a beautiful wife, three lovely children, and an estate in Sleepy Hollow. With all that you have, of what possible use to you is my approval?"

Taken aback, Crane found he could say nothing in response to that.

"Now then," Father said, turning back to Katrina and their daughters, "I assume you have booked passage to that aforementioned estate? I wish to sleep on a floor that does not buck and weave."

"Of course," Katrina said. "Come, Abigail, come, Jennifer."

Crane suddenly lost his footing on the deck. Once again, Jeremy was there to rescue him.

Why did they name their daughters Abigail and Jennifer?

Then he realized that he chose those names because he knew them. Those names were critically important to him in another century. When he died during the war.

But he didn't die, he fought for the whole duration until they achieved victory, and then he and Katrina settled in Sleepy Hollow. He *remembered* this—yet he also remembered being on the battlefield—

—*the masked Hessian faces him, broad axe in hand, rising after Crane shot him. It makes no sense to him, though it is hardly the first nonsensical thing he has encountered these past months. The Hessian isn't even bleeding.*

He swings his axe, slicing through Crane's chest. The pain is agonizing, a line of fire burning through his ribs, and Crane knows he has only moments to act. In a last desperate move before death, he cuts the Hessian's head off. Then he falls to the ground, the blood pouring out of him, intermingling with that of the Hessian as he—

—stumbled again. "This isn't real," he muttered.

"What isn't real, Ichabod?" Katrina asked.

"All of this. I didn't survive the war—yet I lived far beyond it. I was killed, yet I did not die. I slept through Anno Domini 1800, and all the years to follow until I was awakened in the twenty-first century—in which I fight alongside two women named Abigail and Jennifer!"

And then he screamed. . . .

EIGHTEEN

Bronx, New York

—————

JANUARY 2014

"IT AIN'T WORKING!"

That was the last thing Beth wanted to hear Frieda say as she smeared the blood of Al Whitcombe-Sears on the six Independence Crosses. "What's wrong?"

"They're pushin' back, seein' through the illusion'a their heart's desires."

Beth looked up and around the living room. Frank, that lieutenant of his, and some other woman she didn't know were standing at the three entrances to the living room. Each was staring straight ahead, mouths hanging open, arms at their sides.

"All three of them?" Beth asked.

"No, four," Frieda said. "There's another one outside."

"Was wondering where Witness number two was. Why isn't it working? Is it the Agrippa talisman?"

Frieda shook her head. "I ain't sensing the talisman on the one outside. Look, Beth, I *told* you, I'm rusty—I ain't cast nothin' in months!"

Suddenly, Frank, Mills, and the other woman all screamed at the same time and collapsed to the floor. The screams startled Beth as she knelt down by the fifth cross that she had to smear blood on.

Shrugging, Beth said, "That's fine, I'll take it." She smeared blood on the last two crosses, then stood at the center of the sigil she'd drawn on the hardwood. "Keep an eye on them while I cast the spell."

"What the hell do I do if they move?" Frieda asked, but Beth ignored her.

Closing her eyes, she started slowly speaking the words she'd been practicing since October, the words she'd been champing at the bit to cast, just waiting for this eighth half-moon to arrive.

She felt the power of the magic infusing her. Intellectually, she knew that the phases of the moon probably had an effect on the earth's magnetic field and that was what made it possible to cast a particular spell at a particular time.

Ultimately, though, the reasons didn't matter. She just knew it would work.

The words poured out of her mouth, and she could feel the forces swirling about. Everything went away, her living room, Frieda, the three intruders, the house, the neighborhood—there was nothing but Beth, the sigil, the six crosses, the blood, and the magic.

And Serilda.

Beth could feel the mistress, teasing at the edge of her consciousness. Her presence was weak at first, but as she continued to speak the spell, it grew stronger.

At last! After so many centuries of unrest, I may at last return to my rightful place!

Smiling, Beth continued to recite the spell. Serilda's presence was like a warm flannel blanket wrapping around her on a cold winter night.

Already Beth's imagination was running wild with all the things they could accomplish once the mistress was back on the mortal plane.

You have done well, my servant. Rest assured, you will have a place of honor by my side as we remake the world as Abaddon would wish it.

Beth was now halfway through the spell and she wasn't even consciously speaking the words, they seemed to just come from her mouth unbidden.

Nooooooooooooooooo!

Without warning, the flannel blanket was ripped away, leaving Beth cold and confused. Serilda's presence was suddenly fading and less substantial. Beth had to force herself to continue to speak the words of the spell.

And then she felt another presence alongside Serilda. A tall man with a beard wearing a long coat and a poofy shirt.

Gritting her teeth, she forced herself to keep reciting the spell.

. . .

ONCE CRANE SAW through the delusion of his suddenly being a middle-aged man in fin de siècle New York having something resembling a reconciliation with his father, he collapsed to the hard surface of the road.

Struggling to his feet, he cried out in pain, as he rather idiotically used his left hand to brace himself. The self-inflicted cut was still raw and coated in blood.

Shaking it off, Crane steadied himself, cupped the bloodstained Congressional Cross in both hands, and once again began to recite the words of the counterspell.

As he spoke the words, he felt the same chilling winds that accompanied Serilda's presence beneath the armory months ago.

You again! Will I never be free of you, husband of the hated witch?

Crane smiled, but continued to recite the spell. It was Katrina and the rest of her coven who bound Serilda's power, allowing her to be burned at the stake, back in the eighteenth century. And it was Crane, along with Lieutenant Mills, who used old gunpowder to destroy her bones, denying her attempt at resurrection the previous autumn.

I will not allow this! Serilda's words were weaker this time.

Again Crane said nothing save for the words of

the spell. He felt the power coursing through the bloodstained silver of the cross, forcing away the chill cold of Serilda's presence.

When he at last reached the final words of the spell, he cried out, "You will not win this day, Serilda! No matter how murderous your followers, no matter how cruel their attacks, they will not stop us!"

You may be victorious this day, but your woman remains trapped, and she shall stay there evermore!

"Perhaps she shall. But you will not be able to gloat about it any longer."

The Nugent house burst into a mighty glow that temporarily blinded Crane. Raising his hands to shield his eyes, he still saw the glow even with his eyes shut and his arms in the way.

And then the glow faded, and with it, all of Crane's energy. His arms suddenly felt as if they weighed half a ton, he no longer had the capacity to support his own weight, and he once again fell to the ground, struggling mightily to keep his eyes open.

SHAKING HER HEAD, Abbie tried to figure out how she wound up lying on a hardwood floor when she was just in her cubicle. . . .

No, she was just at the Fox Hill Stables. . . .

No, she was here. Standing, facing Nugent as she was about to cast the spell to bring Serilda back when some other woman with scars on half her face walked in.

She was lying next to her Glock, and she gingerly touched it. It was still warm, but much cooler than before, so she grabbed it and then got to her feet.

Quickly, Abbie took stock of the situation. Nugent was lying in the center of the chalk drawing that was in the center of the room. She didn't appear to be moving, and there didn't seem to be any sign of Serilda, which led Abbie to think that Crane had done his part quite admirably.

Irving was still groggily lying on the floor, moaning a bit.

Jenny was on her feet and pointing her weapon right at the head of the scarred woman, who looked understandably apprehensive.

"What the hell did you *do* to me?" That was Jenny, sounding as pissed-off as Abbie had ever heard her. And that was against some mighty fierce competition, given that Jenny had spent most of the past decade being pissed-off.

The scarred woman was whimpering. "I'm sorry, please, don't hurt me."

"You really think 'I'm sorry' is gonna cut it, lady? Do you know what you *did* to me?"

"It was—it was just a harmless spell. Supposed t'let you live your heart's desire. S'why it worked even with the talisman, 'cause it's white magic, not black."

"White magic?" Jenny cocked her pistol, and Abbie flinched.

"Jenny, don't—"

"Shut *up*, Abbie, this doesn't concern you."

"Uhm, it kinda does. Leaving aside the fact that you're, y'know, my sister, there's the fact that you're pointing a weapon at an unarmed woman. That's the sort of thing I'm paid to stop from happening."

"You don't know what she did to me." Jenny had yet to look away from the scarred woman's face, and Abbie saw tears welling up in her eyes.

"I think I can guess. You were living the life you would've lived if we never saw those trees in the forest."

Now, finally, Jenny turned to look at her. She whispered, "You, too?"

Abbie nodded.

She turned back and glared at the scarred woman. "Then you know why I need to shoot her."

"I can't let you do that, Jenny."

"Neither can I."

Abbie glanced behind her to see that Irving had also gotten to his feet. "You okay, Captain?"

"Aside from the herd of elephants running through my head, I'm just peachy. Mills, put the gun down."

"You don't understand!" Jenny cried. "The life she showed me—it was happy and fun and wonderful and I *can't ever have that*!" She shook her head.

"Everything I've been through since that damn night in the forest, and this bitch shows me what it *should've* been like! She has to die for that!"

"Nobody *has* to die, Jenny!" Abbie cried. "Yeah, what she showed us was great—that's what heart's desires are supposed to be. But that's not how it works and you *know* that. We don't get to play what-if. It was just a stupid magic trick trying to keep us from doing what's right—just like every other stupid magic trick we've gone up against the last few months. But the whole point of this is that *we're the good guys,* Jenny!"

At that, Jenny again turned to her sister. Abbie was slowly moving toward her younger sibling, and she saw the look of anguish on her tear-streaked face.

Now standing as close to Jenny as she dared, Abbie lowered her voice, belatedly realizing that Jenny would likely pay more attention if she wasn't yelling. "A lot of people are dead because of what this little coven did. We're supposed to be against that. If we just shoot people because they pissed us off, then why the hell are we bothering to fight Moloch and Serilda and the Horsemen? 'Cause that's the world *they* want. They want death and destruction and pointless suffering."

Jenny looked back at the scarred woman. "But it's not like you can arrest her."

"I can do better'n 'at," the woman said.

"Did anyone say you could talk?" Jenny snapped.

"Jenny!" Abbie then looked at the woman. "Do better than what?"

"I'll testify against Beth. Don't worry," she added quickly, "I'll leave all the magic out, but I heard her talkin' 'bout killin' those folks at the museums. Just *please*," she said with a plaintive look at Jenny, "don't kill me. I thought I could go back to this, I really did, but—" Suddenly, she let out a bitter laugh. "Look at me. Can't even cry, thanks t'Moloch."

Abbie's eyes went wide. "Excuse me? What do you know about Moloch?"

She pointed to the left side of her face. "Who you think did *this*?"

Nodding, Abbie turned to her sister. "Okay, Jenny, c'mon. Put it down."

"You really think that helps?"

"All right, let me put it another way. We're in New York City. Out of Irving's and my jurisdiction. We're in an upscale neighborhood. Trust me, they find a body here, NYPD'll move heaven and earth to find the killer, and Nugent can describe you. Or you wanna kill her, too?"

Abbie watched as Jenny's face went through several different emotions: anger, resentment, confusion, sorrow.

Finally, she lowered her weapon and turned away.

The scarred woman was shaking now. "I'm so sorry. I didn't think—"

"It's okay. We'll take care of you. What's your name?"

"I'm—I'm Frieda. Frieda Abernathy."

"Okay, Frieda, we're gonna have to call the local cops, have them hold you until we can get an arrest warrant. Then you can talk about your deal with the DA. All right?" Abbie refrained from mentioning the jurisdictional nightmare this case would be, as both Westchester County and New York County had claim to Nugent, and given that cops were killed in both counties, neither side would give an inch to the other. But that was a problem for prosecutors and judges to hash out.

Frieda nodded. "That's fine. I—I thought I could just go back to this, and I wasn't gonna, but—" She let out a bitter laugh. "Beth, she gets in your head, y'know? All single-minded. Crazy stuff. She was obsessed."

Irving asked, "Obsessed with what?"

"Serilda. Everything was all about her, all'a time. Crazy stuff," she repeated.

"Damn." Irving shook his head.

Abbie gave him a sympathetic look. This had to have been hard on him. It would've been like her finding out that Corbin was a serial killer. By comparison, the revelation that Corbin was secretly gathering intel on demons and monsters was pretty damn harmless.

Then Abbie looked at Jenny. "You okay?"

She nodded quickly. "Yeah. I mean, no, not really, but okay enough. What'd she hit you guys with?"

"I was with the FBI, and Corbin was still alive."

Irving didn't look at Jenny, but was staring down at the floor when he said, "I was in command of a precinct in Manhattan, Cynthia and I were still married, and Macey could walk."

Jenny winced. "Oh. Oh, damn. I'm sorry, Captain, I—"

"It's okay." Irving waved Jenny off, then looked around. "Where's Crane?"

Abbie also looked around, though of course they left Crane outside on purpose. "I'll check." She moved toward the front door.

As she threw it open, she looked toward the SUV they'd come down in.

Of her fellow Witness, there was no sign. "Crane!" she cried.

Gritting her teeth, she jogged to the car, and again called out, "Crane!"

Then she found him lying facedown on the pavement.

"Dammit!" She ran the rest of the way to him and knelt down. First she checked his pulse, which was thankfully very strong.

A moan escaped Crane's lips, and Abbie let out a huge breath of relief.

She rolled him over and he opened his eyes slowly. "Lieutenant?" he said in a ragged whisper.

She took his hand in hers. "It's okay, Crane. We won. Serilda's not coming back thanks to you."

He smiled. "Thanks to all of us." And then his eyes fluttered.

"Crap." She let go of his hand and whipped out her cell phone to call 911.

NINETEEN

Sleepy Hollow, New York

JANUARY 2014

CRANE STOOD BEFORE the burnt-out ruin of the Whitcombe-Sears Library.

It had been a few days since the incident in Bronck's land, and Crane finally felt well enough to walk more than a few yards without collapsing from sheer exhaustion. The medical technicians who'd examined him outside the Nugent house declared him well but for what they classified as "dehydration," a disease Crane was unfamiliar with. Mills explained that it simply meant he needed to drink more fluids.

Sure enough, Mills joined him. "Good to see you up and around."

"It is good to *be* up and around." He stared at the smoky ruins. "Such a tragic waste."

"Yeah, Drosopoulos and Han were good cops."

"Indeed, as was Mr. Whitcombe-Sears, although I was referring just at the moment to the loss of the library. I remember my grandfather telling me a story he was told by one of his professors at Oxford. There was a fire in the Grandpoole suburb of Oxford in Anno Domini 1671. The professor in question had a home near Sheerlake, and his house contained a huge collection of books." He smiled ruefully and shook his head. "Forgive me—the vision visited upon me by Miss Abernathy has had me thinking of my family. Grandfather always spoke wistfully about all the knowledge that was lost that day."

"Books can be reprinted—or saved online. People, though . . ."

Crane bowed his head, conceding the point. "You are correct, of course, Lieutenant, but you live in an era where books are produced in quantities unheard-of in my own time. Books were not so readily replaced, and knowledge not so easily obtained. And, as we have both learned, knowledge is fickle and not always reliable or findable."

"That's certainly true. C'mon, let's take a walk."

They started to perambulate up Chestnut Street, turning right at Washington Street, which Crane thought apropos.

"At least," he said as they walked south on the street named for Crane's former commanding officer, "we were able to make use of Mr. Whitcombe-Sears's store of knowledge this once. I shudder to think what manner of havoc Serilda might have wrought were she allowed to return to the mortal plane."

"Yeah, that would've sucked." Abbie gave her cheekiest grin, and Crane couldn't help but return it. Then the grin fell. "You never told me what your heart's desire vision was."

Crane had been endeavoring not to dwell on it for the past two days, which meant, naturally, that he could think of little else. So he succinctly shared with Mills the details of his temporarily living the life of an Ichabod Crane who survived the war and raised three children with Katrina.

"Primarily," he concluded, "the vision served to remind me of a horrible truth that I had ill considered up until now. I've no idea how my father reacted to my passing. Did my death on the battlefield fill him with sorrow? Regret? Anger? Righteous smugness?" He shook his head. "Any of those would have been in character, sadly."

"I don't know what to tell you, Crane. What I got from Abernathy was kinda like that. Corbin was the closest thing to a real father I had—and he's gone, too, and I just *wish* he coulda lived to see what's happening. To *help* me."

"Well, to be fair, Lieutenant, he has helped some. His files have proven invaluable."

"Yeah." Mills sighed.

"What of Miss Jenny and Captain Irving?"

"Well, Irving keeps going down to the city for

whatever reason. Dunno if he's visiting his ex and his kid or what. This whole thing's been pretty hard on him. He thought he knew Nugent, y'know?"

Crane nodded. "And Miss Jenny?"

"She's okay." Mills chuckled. "I guess everything she's been through, she rebounds pretty damn good. Then again, she's been getting ready for this fight a lot longer than we have."

To Crane's delight, they found themselves at the northwest corner of Patriots Park.

"Damn, I haven't come over here in ages."

Crane looked down at Mills in surprise. "Indeed? I try to come to this park as often as possible. It is a fine place to think."

"Yeah, well, that's a good reason for me to avoid it. Thinking too much just depresses me lately. Moloch says you'll betray me, Andy Brooks is walking around all zombified, I still don't even know if Jenny's entirely forgiven me for what happened when we were kids, and tomorrow I get to go to the latest in a *series* of cop funerals, which started with my best friend and mentor last fall." She smiled ruefully. "And happy new year to me."

They arrived at the same stone bridge where Crane had met Miss Lianne and her dog Puddles— and where he'd received the vision from Katrina that had gotten them started on the quest to stop Serilda's resurrection.

Mills leaned on the side of the bridge, looking out over the brook flowing noisily under them. "I told Jenny that we're the good guys, that the whole reason we're fighting this fight is to keep the badness from overwhelming the world—but sometimes I look around and wonder if we already lost."

"We *cannot* afford to think that way, Lieutenant," Crane said urgently. "It is when events have turned the most toward despair that we must fight the hardest. For it is giving in to that despair that truly gives our foes their victory. We must cling to what we believe in and what brings us joy. For me, it is the hope that Katrina and I will one day be reunited."

"I guess for me it's to make things right with Jenny."

"I would say you are far closer to your goal than I," Crane said wryly. "In addition, you should be aware that this is far from my first hopeless battle. When I first came to these shores, the colonists' rebellion was considered by my peers to be the height of folly. King George was the mightiest monarch in the world, England held the most land—or so we told ourselves, in any event. The colonists' cause was futile, doomed to failure. They were disorganized, argumentative, untrained—when I arrived in this land, Lieutenant Colonel Tarleton informed me that I would spend only one Christmas in the colonies and that any rebellion would be put down in less than two years' time."

"I'm guessing this Tarleton guy wasn't known for his fortune-telling abilities?" Mills asked.

"Indeed he wasn't."

"Waitasec, isn't he the one who was really a demon?"

Crane nodded. "Perhaps that was the reason for his overconfidence, but his attitude was shared by most of his fellows. Two hundred and fifty years later, those words have been proven fallacious. The upstart colonies have become now what King George's England was then: the greatest power in the world. And all because we did not believe that our cause was lost. That was our greatest strength."

"I guess so. Still, that vision? It was *nice*. I mean, there was the usual bureaucratic nonsense, but still it felt so—so *normal*."

"As was mine—and I suspect Miss Jenny's and Captain Irving's were similarly quotidian—which was why we saw them. The spell that Miss Abernathy cast was one that showed us what we most desired."

"Daydreams. What we hope for, what we dream about. What we wish for." Mills sighed. "But hey, if wishes were horses—"

Crane smiled. "—we would be up to our hips in excrement."

Mills bowed her head. "Exactly. And there's plenty of manure already."

Leaning against the stone next to Mills, Crane just stared out at the brook. For a moment, he closed his eyes—

—and when he opened them, he was once again

in the dark forest with its gnarled trees. The air had once again gone from crisp to thick, and again a half-moon shone in the sky.

But this time there were no visions from his past. Or, rather, there was, but it was simply Katrina, this time wearing the nurse's uniform that she wore the day he and the Horsemen believed they had killed each other.

"I cannot speak to you for long, my love," she said without preamble. "Moloch keeps a greater eye on me these past weeks."

"Lieutenant Mills and I had suspected as much. I must thank you, Katrina: your actions prevented Serilda's rise."

"Hers was always a great evil, and your actions have shattered her coven as well. But I must admit, Ichabod, that what I am most grateful for is not that you prevented Serilda's resurrection," she said with a most uncharacteristically shy smile, "but that you finally were given the laurels you deserved."

"What do you mean?" Crane asked, confused.

"The Congressional Cross. You earned that honor from General Washington himself. It is past time you held it."

She reached out to hold his hand, but she wasn't quite able to reach him so they could touch.

"We will be together soon enough, Katrina," Crane said. "If I can at last be issued my honor from General Washington after two centuries, then we can be together again."

Katrina's smile widened. "We can."

And then Crane was back in Patriots Park.

"Hello? Earth to Crane, come in Crane?"

Blinking, he turned to look at Mills. "I'm sorry?"

"You were on Koozebane there for a minute."

He frowned. "I'm not familiar with that location. How does one get there?"

"Via a very particular street. It's where Kermit the Frog used to report from."

Crane just stared at Mills. "A—a *frog*?"

Mills chuckled. "It'd take too long to explain." She stood upright. "I don't know about you, but I'm starving. How do you feel about a bastardized version of Greek flatbread?"

Crane bowed his head. "I would love to share a pizza with you, Lieutenant. Lead the way to Salvatore's. Or is it Vladimir's?"

"One of those, yeah."

They quit the bridge and continued up toward the Broad Way. As they walked, Crane reached into his coat pocket and took out the Congressional Cross—the only thing besides the *grimoire* that he'd been able to salvage from the Whitcombe-Sears Library. It still had some traces of his blood upon it.

He'd been able to keep it because it wasn't actually in Nugent's possession. The six she did have were currently evidence in her trial and would eventually be returned to their rightful owners. Tilghman's would go back to the Society of the Cincinnati, van Brunt's and Willett's to the Metropolitan Museum of Art, and Cortlandt's to the Cortlandt Museum. Whitcombe's would be donated to the Historical Society serving Sleepy Hollow and Tarrytown, who were the beneficiaries of Mr. Whitcombe-Sears's will—sadly, thanks to the fire, the cross was the only physical item he'd be able to bequeath them, though the society did also get all of his money per that same will.

The sixth cross that Nugent had possession of apparently belonged to another of Serilda's coven, Sophia Cabot, currently in a coma, according to Miss Abernathy. No doubt it would be returned to her family.

Mills noticed him staring at his cross. "Must be nice to finally have something to put on the mantelpiece."

"I suppose I could store it there, yes." Crane hadn't considered where to place it in the cabin he was currently using as his dwelling place.

"Well, you earned it. More than once."

"I suppose so. I just wish the only blood it had cost to obtain it was mine, and not that of so many good people."

"Amen," Mills said quietly.

IN A HOSPITAL bed in Mount Sinai Hospital, a young woman named Sophia Cabot lay, breathing shallowly, several machines attached to various body parts to monitor her vital signs.

She'd been in a coma since the previous October, and the doctors had no prognosis for when, or even if, she would wake up.

Nobody was in the room one fateful January night. It was the first full moon after a half-moon. During the latter, two of Sophia's closest friends attempted to resurrect the mistress whom they all worshipped.

She woke up. And had anyone been in the room when she opened her eyes, they would have seen that those eyes were an obsidian black.

Just like the TV series it's based on, *Sleepy Hollow: Children of the Revolution* mixes historical fact with fantastic fiction in order to tell a grand adventure with Ichabod Crane, Abbie Mills, and the rest in their fight against the forces of darkness.

Patriots Park really does border the towns of Tarrytown and Sleepy Hollow, and is quite lovely. It has all the memorials mentioned in chapter 1, from the dedications to fallen soldiers in World War I, World War II, and the Korean War to the monument to John Paulding and his compatriots who captured Major André.

The story of Lord George Germain's order to the British troops in New York to sail gunboats up the Bronx River has been exaggerated, but while the Regular Army did not try to actually enact Germain's order as legend would have it, his lordship did give it, blissfully unaware that large portions of the river in question are very narrow and shallow. The name "the Bronx" (which is your humble author's birthplace and home) derives from Jonas

Bronck, a Dutch farmer who owned much of the land in the peninsula that now bears his name, hence Crane's references to both river and region by the alternate spelling.

While the Independence Cross (or Congressional Cross) is a fictional award, the others mentioned in the text—the elegant swords issued to ten heroes of the Revolution, the Fidelity Medallion awarded to John Paulding—are actual awards that were issued by the Continental Congress. It's unknown whether the other had magical properties. Independence Cross recipients Tench Tilghman, Henry Knox, and Marinus Willett are all historical personages; Caleb Whitcombe, Ezekiel Cortlandt, and Jebediah Cabot are inventions of the author.

The portrayals of the Metropolitan Museum of Art and the Museum of the City of New York are mostly accurate, with only minor liberties taken, mostly with the security setup of the latter. Also, there really is a gallery in the American Wing of the Met with a portrait of Marinus Willett catty-corner from a portrait of Washington, and it really is in the next room over from Leutze's portrait of Washington crossing the Delaware. If you're ever in New York City, I highly recommend both museums—in particular, the Astor Court at the Met is even more magnificent than described here (mostly because words cannot possibly do justice to the place). However, the Cortlandt Museum in Tarrytown and the Whitcombe-Sears Library in Sleepy Hollow are both wholly fictional.

The Society of the Cincinnati was formed in 1783 by the aforementioned Henry Knox, and included officers of the Continental Army and the French army and navy. George Washington was the society's first president general. Originally a society of noble soldiers, who passed on their membership to their firstborn sons, these days it's an educational nonprofit organization. Their museum is located at Anderson House in Washington, D.C. The traveling exhibit that lands at MCNY is wholly a creation of the author.

Washington's famous crossing of the Delaware River on Christmas night in 1776 was indeed to fight Hessian mercenaries who held Trenton for the British. While the public story that he wished to achieve a victory after the demoralizing retreat from New York that is in the history books is accurate, it was also a full moon that night (it's how Washington and his troops were able to see to cross the treacherous river), and we all know how important moon phases are to witches. Lieutenant Colonel Johann Rall was indeed the commandant of the Hessians in Trenton, and anecdotally, he was given a note saying that Washington was approaching, which he then shoved in his pocket unread; some say he was eating dinner, some say he was playing chess, few say he was summoning the demon Abaddon to infuse its power into a woman named Serilda. The note was, however, found on his body after he was shot—that it was Washington who shot him is an indulgence of the author.

Abaddon is a name that has been associated with one of the angels present at the apocalypse and with a demon of fire, so that connection to Serilda, who burns her victims, is a stronger connection than the language of the Romany, especially since the name derives from the term "to destroy."

Martha Washington's mother and brother did both die in 1785, though the exact causes are lost to history. And there really and truly was an annular eclipse on 4 August 1785, which was followed by a new moon on the fifth.

The Ticonderoga Police Department really does use the rank of "investigator" rather than "detective," which is actually kind of cool. The portrayal of the fort is also accurate, and yes, there really is a sewage plant in the same shape as, though a much smaller size than, the fort. The locals have a nickname for it that's not appropriate for a family novel. The Liberty Monument is indeed at the intersection of Wicker and Montcalm, and it's quite nifty. (Right alongside it is the Hancock House, a replica of the Beacon Hill mansion of Thomas Hancock, uncle of John Hancock.)

The Tappan Zee Bridge's history as related by Abbie is an accurate, if abbreviated, summary of the span's origins, and construction has begun on a new bridge just north of the current one, which links Tarrytown and Nyack. The replacement bridge is scheduled to open in 2018. A proposal is under consideration to name the new bridge after the great folk singer Pete Seeger, who died in early 2014.

There was a blood moon on 8 October 2013, which is likely when the *Sleepy Hollow* episode "Blood Moon" took place. The first half-moon of January 2014 was eight half-moons after that date.

Google Maps will tell you to take Interstate 87 to drive from Sleepy Hollow to the northwest section of the Bronx, but locals are more likely to take the Saw Mill River Parkway for two reasons: there's a toll on 87 (only seventy-five cents, but still), and the Saw Mill is a prettier drive. Yes, there are a few traffic lights on the latter, but it's worth it for the more pleasant scenery. (In terms of time, the two are pretty much the same.)

Heinrich Cornelius Agrippa von Nettsheim was a writer, physician, theologian, astrologer, soldier, and more, who published several books on the occult in the sixteenth century. He is credited with popularizing the notion of a pentagram as a symbol of magic in Renaissance Europe, and there are people in modern times who still use Agrippa pentagrams to ward off black magic (including Sheriff Corbin).

There was indeed a fire in the Grandpoole region of Oxford on 25 April 1671, which started in a workhouse belonging to a shoe smith, and also destroyed several tan houses, malt houses, and stables, as well as about seventeen different homes—including, apparently, that of one of the professors under whom Crane's grandfather studied.

Finally, *Children of the Revolution* takes place between the first-season *Sleepy Hollow* episodes "The Golem" (which took place shortly before Christmas) and "The Vessel" (which took place after the new year). The reader is asked to assume that, after taking her around the Metropolitan Museum of Art in chapter 2, Irving took Macey to the adjoining Central Park, where Irving had his fateful encounter with the possessed vendor in "The Golem." The business he had to take care of in New York City in addition to guarding the Independence Cross in the Museum of the City of New York in chapter 8 was to request that the vendor and other folks in the park be questioned, as they were in "The Vessel."

ACKNOWLEDGMENTS

Primary thanks must go to Meagan Stacey, my delightful editor, who was the one who came to me with the notion of doing a *Sleepy Hollow* novel (which I accepted heartily), and who guided this book through to its published state. Secondary thanks also to Meagan's fabulous assistant Kim Silverton, my superb agent Lucienne Diver, the book's excellent publicist Lauren Kuhn, and the fine folks at Fox who provided excellent feedback at the outline and manuscript stage.

Huge thanks to my dear friend Carol Provoncha, who gave me a lovely tour of the reconstructed Fort Ticonderoga, and who was a valuable resource for the scenes taking place at the fort and its environs.

Special thanks to the actors who have given form and substance to the characters portrayed herein: Tom Mison, Nicole Beharie, Katia Winter, Lyndie Greenwood, Neil Jackson, Jill Marie Jones, Amandla Stenberg, John Cho, Michael Roark, Victor Garber, the great Clancy Brown, and the mighty Orlando Jones. Also thanks to Alex Kurtzman, Roberto Orci, Phillip Iscove, and Len Wiseman, who created this wonderful show, and the many writers who have guided it with them, notably Melissa Blake, Mark Goffman, Damian Kindler, Jose Molina, and Heather V. Regnier.

More thanks to friends and family who were incredibly supportive: Wrenn Simms, Tina Randleman, Dale Mazur, Neal Levin, Laura Anne Gilman, Meg Nuge, and especially GraceAnne Andreassi DeCandido (aka The Mom). And, of course, the pets: Scooter, Kaylee, and Louie, as well as the late great Belle and Sterling.

Keith R. A. DeCandido has now, with this novel, written in twenty-five different licensed universes. He doubts it's a record, but it makes for a great line to drop at cocktail parties, which he'll start doing as soon as someone invites him to one. His other tie-in fiction includes books, comics, short fiction, role-playing games, and more based on other TV shows (*Star Trek, Leverage, Doctor Who, Supernatural*), movies (*Cars, Kung Fu Panda, Resident Evil, Serenity*), games (World of Warcraft, Dungeons and Dragons, StarCraft, BattleTech), and comic books (*Spider-Man, X-Men, Hulk, Silver Surfer*). In 2009, he was awarded a Lifetime Achievement Award by the International Association of Media Tie-in Writers, so he never needs to achieve anything ever again. Keith also has several works he keeps the copyright on, including the series of fantasy police procedurals that started with *Dragon Precinct* and includes *Unicorn Precinct, Goblin Precinct, Gryphon Precinct, Mermaid Precinct,* and *Tales from Dragon Precinct;* various and sundry urban fantasy short stories set in Key West, Florida, many of which were collected in *Ragnarok and Roll: Tales of Cassie Zukav, Weirdness Magnet;* and the novels *SCPD: The Case of the Claw* and *Guilt in Innocence: A Tale of the Scattered Earth*. His other recent work includes *Star Trek: The Klingon Art of War;* an adventure in the *Firefly* role-playing game Echoes of War; an essay in *New Worlds and New Civilizations: Exploring Star Trek Comics;* the short story collection *Without a License: The Fantastic Worlds of Keith R. A. DeCandido*; and short stories in the anthologies *Stargate: Far Horizons, V-Wars* volumes 1 and 3, *Bad-Ass Faeries: It's Elemental, With Great Power,* and *Out of Tune*. His twice-weekly rewatch of *Star Trek: Deep Space Nine* can be found on Tor.com; he did a similar rewatch of *The Next Generation* for the site from 2011 to 2013. When he isn't writing, Keith is also a freelance editor for clients both corporate and personal, the percussionist for the parody band Boogie Knights, a second-degree black belt in karate, a prolific podcaster (The Chronic Rift, HG World, Gypsy Cove, The Dome, and his own Dead Kitchen Radio), and a devoted follower of the New York Yankees. He lives in the Bronx with assorted humans and animals. Find out less at his cheerfully retro website at DeCandido.net, which is the gateway to his various bits of online and social media presence, thus simplifying the tasks of cyberstalkers everywhere.

"BONKERSAWESOME, EXCITING, FUNNY, SWEET, EMOTIONALLY INTELLIGENT AND WONDERFULLY SATISFYING"
– THE HUFFINGTON POST
SLEEPY HOLLOW
THE COMPLETE FIRST SEASON
OWN IT ON BLU-RAY™ DVD AND DIGITAL HD
LOADED WITH HOURS OF BONUS FEATURES INCLUDING EXCLUSIVE EXTRAS.
© 2014 Twentieth Century Fox Home
TWENTIETH CENTURY FOX, FOX and associated logos are trademarks of Twentieth Century Fox Film Corporation and its related entities.